# The Vampire Patrons

# The Vampire Patrons

A Vampire Comedy
Legal Thriller

Robert Gruett

Dedicated to Kelli, a good friend and my first inspiration.

You allowed me to take writing seriously before
I understood what it meant to be a writer.

I finally did it.  Now it's your turn.

# ~ ACKNOWLEDGMENTS ~

In August of 2007, Andy Meisenheimer gave an interview in which he was asked what types of manuscripts he would be seeking while attending an upcoming writers' conference. His answer: comic vampire legal thrillers.

Two years later, while dealing with a serious case of writer's block, I decided to take up his challenge. Of course, at the time I had no idea that what would start out as an amusing diversion from my heavyweight projects would soon take on a life of its own, becoming not only my first novella and published book, but also one of the most enjoyable projects I have worked on to date.

So, Andy, thank you for keeping your sense of humor about you during that interview. If you hadn't, this book would never have been written.

A big thanks to Brian and Suzanne for risking a great many brain cells by being the first to tread the waters of this story, and to Erin for lending to me her proofreading expertise.

My love to Emerald, who brings me far more joy than I often show – I am so proud of you – and to little David, whose endless smiles have kept me going during many difficult days.

A very special thanks to my wonderful wife, Liane. No matter how I have faltered, your grace and encouragement have never ceased. You are my anchor, my light, and my love.

I'll do the thing with the book, and God does the rest, right?

# ◦✦ ℙ ROLOGUE ✦◦

The single greatest misconception held by the general public concerning vampires isn't that we sleep in coffins, that we can't enter your home without an invitation, or that we're likely to turn into bats and flit into the night at the first sign of a crucifix-wielding priest. No, the single most mistaken belief is something far more disturbing: the notion we can't appreciate a good joke.

Sure, I'll admit we lean toward the serious side, and back in the Middle Ages we were wrapped up in capes and castles and candlelit ceremonies, but then, the rest of you were obsessed with pitchforks and torches and chasing hysterical mobs through our living rooms. Still, time has changed us all, and those half-crazed farmers with nothing better to do than harass some poor fool who forgot to raise the castle drawbridge for the night are now businessmen and politicians. Progress changed us as well. I'd even go so far as to say it's civilized us – well, most of us anyway: my brother Jacob went to college and came back a lawyer, but there's a black sheep in every family.

He's the exception, of course. I have a sister as well. Annie went to law school and works the homicide beat downtown. She's been trying to make it into paranormal investigations for a while now, but despite her sixth sense in the field she hasn't managed to get her foot in the door yet.

When it comes to the family business, Freddie's the respectable one, although his dedication to our more eccentric traditions keeps him away from mainstream 21$^{st}$ century life. But he's nothing if not entertaining, and we give him the family therapy he craves while he pays us back with the amusement that can only come from a sibling who happens to be both vampire and not right in the head.

Then there's me. I'm a comedian.

Well, that's not entirely true.

Actually, it's in no way true. I'd like to be one, but the nuisances of life seem to have made it their goal to place themselves squarely in my way. You know the type: mortgage payments, a full-time job, preparing for the inevitable zombie apocalypse – the usual stuff. Suffice to say I practice my art only on a single audience these days, and only because we meet every Thursday evening at Barlowe's for dinner.

I'm not sure who came up with the idea, and I couldn't care less as long as we keep doing it; it gives me a chance to try out new material over a second-rate meal in the company of an only slightly dysfunctional family.

What more could one possibly want? A lycan named Larry to wait our table?

We have one of those too.

# CHAPTER ONE

## APRIL 15ᵀᴴ

When I arrived at Barlowe's, I was already an hour late and soaking wet, and while I wish I could have chalked it up to a gang of mischievous garden gnomes or a bad-tempered pixie – each would have provided a passable excuse – the cause of my trouble was something far worse: a gremlin. And not the sort that climbs inside machinery and wreaks havoc on its inner workings, though I wouldn't be surprised if that was just the sort of skullduggery afoot on the assembly line.

No, I'm talking about my '71 Gremlin.

When I bought it off a used car lot ten years back, I'd convinced myself that where its reliability failed, its looks would prevail, a decision I've spent the last nine years trying to forget. Nights like tonight, when the engine's dead and the raindrops are coming down in twos just for kicks, I find that delusion as impossible as my career choice.

"Problems with the Gremlin?" Annie briefly raised her face from her newspaper to take in my waterlogged state.

"No, why do you ask?" I collapsed into my regular seat beside her own, snatched up a napkin and wiped it across my dripping face, then grabbed for the nearest menu. "What's good tonight?"

"You order the same thing every week," Jacob mumbled, frowning over a cup of coffee from across the table. He didn't even bother looking up as he peered down through a pair of reading glasses and into the open pages of a thick book set beside his place setting. "Why even bother asking?"

"Because it adds to my mystique." I find when you don't have a rational answer to give, sarcasm works equally well.

If you can pull it off.

I can't.

Annie stifled a laugh. "There's *nothing* mysterious about you, except maybe your profession. How's the comedy circuit?"

"Top Down isn't looking for any new talent, The Happy Hobgoblin is booked for the next twelve months, and I can't get any of the major theatres to pick up my act. For now I'm stuck hand-holding executives who don't know the difference between Bluetooth and blogging."

"Hmmm," Jacob sat back, lowering his coffee and getting comfortable. "You know, I have some pull with our firm's IT manager, and he's looking to fill a vacancy."

Annie coughed. We glanced at her. "Bad idea," she mouthed the words silently.

Jacob rolled his eyes. "Like I was saying, I could get the two of you connected."

"Right," I answered. "Sorry, but if I have to choose between an idiot supervisor with nothing but ego where his brains should be and the most noble lawyer on the planet, I'll stick with my current lot any day of the week."

"Bad idea," Annie mumbled. "Did I mention?"

"Pay's got to be a step up," Jacob added.

"Probably, but right now I'm the big fish in the pond, and it's a casual pond where the company buys lunch every Friday, and I'm close enough to dash home for a nap if things are slow."

"Suit yourself," Jacob returned his attention to his reading material, his interest in the whole idea apparently lost.

"Have you read this?" Annie asked, putting her paper down and tapping her finger on an article. "The mayor is considering assembling a special police force to deal with the rising number of maulings on the streets. Apparently, the top brass is already on board."

"Maulings?" I asked. It didn't ring a bell, but then it wouldn't. I avoid most media, so I'm usually a bit behind when it comes to the latest news. Maybe that's one of the reasons my stand-up is so poor; I find it rather relies on a vague awareness of current events, not to mention one's general surroundings. I tend to fail in both respects.

"Yes, maulings," Annie repeated. "People being killed and torn apart in back alleys late at night. Been going on for months now. Lycanthropes, from the sound of it."

"Demographic?" Jacob asked, sipping away.

"Not much to go on. Older individuals. Men and women both. Rich. Recently divorced or married. All humans." She propped her elbow up on the table and rested her head in an upturned hand. "Not sure if that constitutes a trend or not."

"You could ask Larry," I offered. "He's gotten you the inside track more than once before."

Larry was our waiter.

Our regular waiter.

In fact, in two years of Thursday night dinners at Barlowe's we'd never been served by anyone else. He'd gotten to know us well. So well, in fact, that not only had he memorized each of our usuals long ago, he could tell by our demeanor alone which we intended to order.

He was also a werewolf.

Now to an important point: vampires and werewolves don't get along.

At all.

Except, apparently, on Thursday nights at bad restaurants when one is waiter, the other patron, and a tip is involved.

Other than that, we generally loathe, hunt, and kill each other.

It's nothing personal; it's just nature's way of reminding us that some things weren't meant to coexist: fire and ice, Democrats and Republicans, pro wrestling and IQs over fifty.

You get the idea.

Larry was a good guy. At least, he'd always been straight with us, and over time we'd developed a mutual respect for each other. Freddie had his own thoughts, I'm sure, but the rest of us would almost certainly have let him walk if we passed him in a dark alley on a quiet night.

Probably.

"I don't know," Annie answered. "As long as Detective Gayton is running the show, I doubt many of my own leads will make it to the chief's desk."

"Now that's a defeatist attitude," Jacob answered, his tone suddenly one of lecturing schoolmaster as he pulled off his glasses for added emphasis.

I groaned. He's the oldest of all of us, and his profession as an attorney not withstanding, he sees himself as something of a role model for the rest of us.

In this case he was probably right.

"Look," he continued, "you've been trying to get yourself noticed for the past year now, pushing to get into paranormals. This could be your chance. Now if you have an inside source, you'd be foolish to pass it by, especially when your force's reputation is on the line. A reputation that has fallen into disrepute in recent months. A reputation you," and he raised a single eyebrow for effect, "might well save."

He lifted his mug and took another sip – no, a slurp, and quickly extinguished the mood he intended to create.

Annie nodded slowly, lost in thought. "I suppose."

"Excellent," I announced, then raised my hand and snapped my fingers in my best dramatic pose. "*LARRY!*"

In any other restaurant, with any other waiter, that probably would have been considered rude. But not at Barlowe's and not at our table. The staff and customers had grown used to our brand of entertainment long ago, and mine in particular. I like to think they looked forward to it week after week.

I was probably wrong, but no need to dwell on that.

Immediately, a large man appeared beside our table. Now, when I say large, I mean very large, unreasonably large, *offensively* large: six and a half feet and bulky, and all of it muscle. Hairy muscle. Furry, even. He shaved, sure, but the telltale scruff was there: a thick mantle of bronze hair, bristles of afternoon shadow crawling across his face and down his neck to vanish beneath a white collar. To an unaware bystander, he may have passed for anyone with an addiction to weight-lifting and a healthy fear of razors, but we knew better.

Larry was all lycan, head to toe, inside and out. We didn't even need to look. We could smell the wild blood in his veins. Just as he no doubt sensed the chill in ours.

"Gentlemen," he smiled wide, his teeth sharp and white, "and ladies," he added, nodding in Annie's direction. Then he clasped his hands together and leaned in close. "As usual, I would offer to present to you tonight's selections, but I can see that each of you have decided already. Therefore, I will be ordering one filet mignon in a light sauce with a glass of Merlot for the lawyer; a burger, no onions, with a side of waffle fries and a water for the detective; and a Smashing Spaghetti off the kids menu with a cola for our resident aspiring comedian."

"Uh, not tonight," I answered him. The thought of marinara turned my stomach. In fact, it was less the sauce and more the thought of anything liquid and red.

Odd thing for a vampire to feel, actually.

"I beg your pardon?" Larry rose back to his full height, eyeing me with a curious stare.

"Not really in the mood, that's all. Do you have anything a little less zesty? Maybe some chicken fingers or something?"

"Of course. I will see to it." He grew thoughtful for a moment. "Oh, and one more thing," he addressed us all.

"What is it?" Annie asked.

"It's your brother. He's outside."

"Thank you. Please invite him in," then she added, "*All* the way in."

Larry nodded and left, a few long strides taking him briskly out of sight. Annie sighed.

"You know," Jacob mused, "We could just leave him out there."

"Jacob!" she scolded.

But he only shrugged. "It's his own fault, you know. No one makes him follow the old rules, and if you pay attention you'll notice he's even added a few of his own. For crying out loud, he can't even go to the bathroom without one of us going in first."

"It's his way."

"It's idiotic. Even Father thought so."

"Don't go dragging Dad into this," I interrupted. "There's one in every family."

"Two in some," Jacob mumbled.

I wasn't sure how to take that.

Probably better not to try.

Now, as I've already said, Freddie's the respectable one, or more precisely, the traditional one. If there's a myth associated with vampires, practical or not, he lives by it.

What do I mean?

Well, for starters, he sleeps in a coffin. Ridiculous, I know, but no more so than his unwillingness to cross over running water, making travel difficult, especially in a city with so many bridges.

Then there's his aversion to crosses, and I'm not just talking about your standard crucifix – any two perpendicular overlapping lines are enough to send him into a panic, but only when one's horizontal and the other's vertical. Apparently, angles don't count. On a windy afternoon last year, the four of us drove out of town and ended up along a road dotted with old European-style windmills, the kind with four blades instead of three. Of course we didn't foresee the obvious danger in this plan until we were a good mile along, at which point Freddie, who could stand it no longer, found himself obliged to stutter back and forth between relaxed and terrified so quickly and eagerly that we thought for sure he'd gone into a seizure.

He also avoids sunlight like the French avoid bathing. Sure, the worst it'll do is give him a minor sunburn, but so what? Vampires and sunlight aren't supposed to go together, so he conducts his affairs nocturnally.

And then there's the matter of entering a home, a room, a car, pretty much anything with a door. They're all off-limits unless someone else goes in first and asks him in. That's why his own home has no doors – no front, no rear, no bedroom doors, no closet doors, not even doors on the kitchen cabinets. And as Jacob pointed out, even a public bathroom stall requires special attention, a point of particular infuriation for the rest of us. There's nothing worse than putting yourself between a bad-tempered, diarrheal vampire and the porcelain object of his deliverance, although it's not so much getting in first that's the problem; it's getting back out before the finale that's the real trick.

That was the reason for Annie's added instruction to Larry. A few months prior, the hostess on duty had invited him in from the sidewalk but neglected to call him into the establishment proper. He spent the next hour wandering around the entryway for a summons that never came. After that, we made certain the staff understood his special needs.

Freddie made his grand entrance at last, shuffling around the corner with head back and chin out, probably to hide his dark, combed-back hair and widow's peak until due emphasis called for its appearance. But that would pose no shock to the other guests, who were no doubt already taken in by his glistening black cape and upturned collar, a garment which he wore over his shoulders and folded hands like a king's mantle.

Which reminds me, despite all his quirks, there's one thing about Freddie we've all grown to appreciate: in his quest to uphold himself as the classic vampire exemplar, he habitually mimics whichever famous bloodsucker he's last had the fortune to catch on TV. I know that because he doesn't read books and we bought him a subscription to Pay-Per-View last Christmas. All those channels and what does he watch? Bela Lugosi.

I didn't even know you could get that sort of thing on demand.

The point is that one week he'll show up looking like Count Dracula, and the next, Grandpa Munster. We've even had the pleasure of The Lost Boys joining us for dinner on occasion.

And yes, I do mean all of them.

But it's nothing if not entertaining, and so long as we steer him clear of the Buffy franchise, we've agreed to let this eccentric addiction of his slide.

He more glided than walked to his seat, and there he paused, dipped his head disdainfully downward, rolled his eyes at what he obviously considered an inferior throne for his classy vampiric backside, and sat slowly down, maintaining a monolithic pose through it all. Then he went and ruined it all by adjusting himself, shifting his weight from one hind quarter to the other, then back again, then spinning sideways and elevating his crossed legs upon the corner of the table, then down again, coming at last to rest face-forward with hands clutching the arms of the chair, his long black fingernails biting into the wood, and his bowed head scorning over his place setting.

"Pitiful," he hissed through teeth far sharper than ours, and if I wasn't mistaken, more plastic as well.

"And what is that?" Jacob asked in a disinterested tone.

"Simply pitiful." Not much of a response, but at least he'd spoken his mind.

That was a start.

"How are you, Frederick?" Annie asked, reaching out across the table to take his hand. "How are things?"

He ignored the gesture, though his eyes found her hand before slowly crawling up her arm to her face. "Pitiful."

"So who are you idolizing tonight?" I asked. "You look like you've got the whole Dracula thing going on, but I'm not really feeling the accent."

"It is not every question that deserves an answer," he replied, tilting his head in my direction, the widow's peak making its formal appearance at last.

"Publius Syrus." Jacob spoke up.

"How do you do that?" Annie asked in astonishment.

"It's a hobby," Jacob answered.

"More importantly," I interrupted, "where does Freddie get his quotes from?" I turned back to the newcomer with an inquiring gaze.

He returned it, albeit with greater boredom than I recall sending his way, but he said nothing.

"Well?" I asked.

"No answer is also an answer."

"That's an old Danish saying," Jacob spouted off again. "And to answer your question, I bought him a Quotationary for his birthday. Broadening of horizons and all that."

"Right," I replied. "Did it come on DVD?"

Our meal was strangely quiet for once, an oddity worthy of closer study had my mind not been so occupied with my stomach's futile attempts at digesting my poor dinner choice. I really must give Larry his due – he's nothing if not knowledgeable when it comes to our selections, and if I'd listened to him when I had the chance, maybe I wouldn't have a long night of sprinting to the bathroom to look forward to.

Oh, well. Next week I'll probably listen.

Probably.

# CHAPTER TWO

## APRIL 22^(ND)

I arrived for dinner early, hoping to make up for my late arrival the previous week, but my plans to impress were cut short when I found Jacob already seated and striking his usual pose, coffee in one hand as he stared down upon a heavy book set wide upon the table below.

"You're early," he said, unimpressed with my show of punctuality.

"It's empty in here," I commented, glancing around at the empty booths on all sides. Barlowe's never did reach full capacity unless there was a convention going on in one of the hotels down the street, but tonight the restaurant was a certified ghost town.

"It's always empty this time of the day."

"And you're here this time every week?"

"Most weeks. Annie too. She's due any minute, so be careful."

"What do you mean?"

He smiled slightly, never once taking his eyes off his reading material, and seemed for a moment to consider whether or not to pass along the explanation. "She rarely arrives in a good mood. Takes her a while to let go of the day, you understand. As a matter of fact," and he looked up suddenly, leaning to the side to look past my shoulders, "here she comes now. Get ready."

He was right. I heard her long before she appeared, her approach from behind announced by the clap of angry heels, and I briefly considered the wisdom in sitting with my back to the door. But before I knew it, she'd slapped a newspaper across the table and was gouging an article with her fingernail.

The article probably had it coming.

"Have you read this?" she demanded, scowling at me.

I shook my head.

She should have known better than to ask.

"More trouble with the media?" Jacob asked without any real interest. He knew the routine.

"And who are they smearing? *Again?*"

"The force." He knew the routine well.

"The force," she parroted, dropping into her own chair and folding her arms.

Jacob took it from there, setting his coffee aside, putting down his glasses, and folding his hands upon the table. "You can't really be that surprised. Public trust *has* waned since Mayor Blackburg took office. And these murders on the street are giving the critics a new excuse to trot out their old guns. You can't blame them for feeling not enough is being done."

"First of all, they're maulings, not simple murders. There's a difference. And second, they could at least stick to the topics." She turned back to me. "You know what they're griping about now?"

I shook my head.

She *really* should have known better than to ask.

"The zombie squads."

The reference came up blank. My face must have shown it.

"You know? The bomb squad replacements?"

"I don't follow." I really didn't.

Annie sighed an exasperated sigh, then took it from the top. "Over the past six months, the mayor has been working with the chief of police to roll out a test bomb squad program, replacing all the humans on the squads with zombies."

"What for?"

"What else? To save money. They figure it'll be cheaper to let zombies blow themselves up trying to disarm bombs than to pay for all the training and protection necessary to have a human do the job. It's all PR, since the governor promised during the last election to do something about the undead camps that have been cropping up all over the state, and now it's time to make good on his word."

"Yes, it's PR, and bad PR if you ask me," Jacob piped up. "The mayor should know better than to rile the zombie rights activists."

"Zombie rights?" I chuckled. "That's absurd."

"Don't laugh. I hear France is about to put a zombie on their presidential ticket."

Leave it to the French.

It was bad enough they threw up the white flag when the mimes invaded back in the 1800s. But now they have to go and surrender to the next worst thing: zombie political correctness.

They should have stopped while they were behind.

Then again, there could be upsides: a zombie wouldn't require the sort of 24/7 protection a human president would need, a zombie probably wouldn't be caught having an affair with an intern, and a zombie wouldn't require first class travel accommodations – the boot of a car would do as nicely as a private jet.

And a zombie would definitely get along with its government counterparts, what with its passive attention to anything not involving brains and your average politician's natural defense in a lack thereof.

Only kidding – zombies don't really eat brains. They're more into stinky cheese.

Not unlike the French, actually.

Maybe they've got things figured out after all.

"Well, I don't agree with the new squads either," Annie reeled me back to reality, "but we're spread thin enough as it is, and I can't say I don't understand the chief's interest in bringing them on board."

"Really?" Jacob replied, his tone only slightly mocking. "Has there been a sudden upswing in bomb threats that's somehow eluded the papers?"

"Of course not. But those on the roll are being redeployed to other assignments."

"Redeployed where?" I asked.

"Well, there's the new blood bank that just opened downtown, and of course the Marx Casino just a block north of that. And with these maulings we need to establish a greater presence on the streets, especially at night."

"Sorry," I interrupted, "but don't the blood bank and casino hire out private security?"

She snickered. "Rent-A-Cops? Yeah, right. Those kids wouldn't last a day in this town, and they cost a lot more than black-and-whites anyway. Plus, things tend to get messy when they're around. "

"So they're expensive and incompetent, and the police have to pick up the slack?"

"Let's just say that once again Blackburg's bit off more than he can chew, and now it's up to us to keep the peace. But the casino is supposed to be a big moneymaker for the city, and they've promised to subsidize our payrolls. As for the blood bank, it's federal, but our mayor's struck a deal to provide shared security." She sat back in her chair, exhaling loudly. "It's all about the money."

Of course, the blood bank Annie mentioned wasn't a blood bank in the traditional sense. Rather, it was a medical plant, one specializing in the conversion of healthy human blood into a medicinal form, specifically plasma platelets: extracted, dehydrated, and concentrated into a pill to be swallowed whole in as civilized a manner as anyone could expect. We in the vampire community have come to think of it as our medicine, and while it may sound distasteful, it's better than the alternative. Without it, life would be much more exciting.

Just as it was before the Blood Laws.

"It's *always* about the money," Jacob replied. "In fact, I've been trying for a while now to convince our brother here that there's more to life than being happy. But apparently wealth doesn't mean to him what it means to the rest of the world."

"Don't start on the whole career thing again," I cut him off. "I like being where I'm at."

"You're in a rut."

"Is it wrong to stick with a job just because I enjoy it?"

"It's wrong because it's lazy. And you're not doing what you really want to be doing anyway, so there goes *any* argument for staying put. As long as you're not performing stand-up, you might as well come work at the firm."

"I've already told you I have no interest in a stuffy office filled with legal bookworm sleazebags."

"You should know we're not all sleazebags."

"Right. Most of you aren't much more than slime balls."

"With a wit like that, I can't believe they're not clamoring to get you onstage."

"Enough!" Annie's voice cut the air like an angry knife, bringing an abrupt end to what was shaping up to be a promising, if not juvenile, quarrel.

"Ah, excuse me," a deep voice prompted us to turn, and there we saw Larry, his hulking form towering just feet away, though none of us had noticed his arrival until just then. He held in his hands a small order pad, a pen at the ready.

"Sorry about that," Annie apologized. "They're like children."

"Nothing to worry about," he answered. Then, rather abruptly, he stepped forward and squatted down on one knee, leaning in close. "Actually, I overheard you talking, and I was wondering if I might offer up some information."

Jacob chuckled. "Information? Would this information be, shall we say, *unconventional* for a person in your line of work?"

Larry smiled. I thought there was more to it than amusement.

"Very much so," he replied. "As a matter of fact, it concerns the attacks to which the papers have been giving so much attention lately."

Annie's jaw dropped. "The maulings? Don't tell me you know something!"

He glanced quickly around before returning his gaze to us. "The lycans are not involved."

"Well, of course you'd say that," Jacob scoffed. "No offense, Larry, but do you really expect us to take *your* word for it?"

Larry ignored him. "They are meant to appear as lycan attacks, but those responsible are clearly not werewolves."

"How do you know?" Annie asked.

"I know."

"*How* do you know?"

He eyed her, and I sensed he was not comfortable sharing any more information than was absolutely necessary. "For one, the injuries are all wrong. Too many cuts, not enough of them vital. Lycans don't play with their victims, and so far not a single casualty seems capable of putting up a fight. So whoever is committing these murders doesn't understand the way lycans think. Or," and he sent a suspicious eye around the table, "how good we are at killing."

"That's it?" Jacob asked. "Lycans are better at murder than we give them credit for, so they couldn't possibly be involved?"

"There is also the fur."

"Trace amounts have been found embedded in the wounds and around the bodies," Annie nodded. "What about it?"

"Has your forensics tested it?"

"Of course."

"And?"

Annie shrugged. "It's werewolf fur."

He frowned. "Hmmm... Have them test it again. And this time, tell them to compare it to this." He reached into his pocket and withdrew a small plastic bag, its contents a mass of dark fuzz.

"What's this?" she asked, taking it.

"That's your control."

"That's yours?" I asked, surprised and somewhat disgusted.

He turned to me. "Would you like me to tell you where I pulled it from?"

"If it's the same I find at the bottom of my dinners week after week, I'm going to go ahead and assume it came from the most hygienic part of you, thanks." Just saying it made me feel dirty. I quickly doused my mouth with a glass of ice water.

"You know," Jacob piped up again, "for a restaurant with a plaque from the sanitation department hanging behind the front desk, you certainly don't mind flaunting your habits in front of the patrons, do you?"

Larry gave him a dirty look. "You could thank me."

"That would require me believing you, which I don't. Not that I think you're lying outright," and he raised his hands in a show of innocence. "But really, you can't not see the irony in a werewolf defending his fellow werewolves."

"Irony would be a vampire defending a werewolf. But I don't suppose that comes up in your line of work, does it?"

Jacob's face, already void of amusement, somehow grew more so. "I'm a prosecutor. I don't make a habit of defending *anyone*. If I did, I'd be out of a job."

Larry smirked and slowly returned to his full height. "Then I won't take anything you have to say personally."

"Or seriously," I added. "Just a suggestion."

"Well, since you two are clearly about to get back to it, may I ask if your brother will be joining us tonight?"

Annie looked at Jacob.

Jacob looked at me.

I looked at my watch, which was really irrelevant to the matter entirely. I had no idea if Freddie was going to show up or not, but since the majority had elected me resident expert on the matter, and since just then I was a good deal more preoccupied with the disturbingly vacant state of my stomach than matters of family etiquette, I said, "Nope, I don't think so."

"Very well." And with that Larry droned off into his intrepid round of weekly culinary recommendations, which, I might add, I took to heart willingly. After the events of the previous week, I fully intended to get a full night of sleep tonight.

I've come to observe that our Thursday nights together tend to follow a certain pattern. We arrive, one at a time. We talk, but talk inevitably turns to arguing before we've had a chance to order. Once those pleasantries are out of the way, Larry shows up to tell us what we want to eat, but that's just an intermission, giving us each a chance to formulate new and illogical arguments to use against the others. When he leaves we're back at it until the food arrives, and then it's all small talk. At any point during these proceedings, Freddie may or may not show up — it's really anyone's guess, as is his persona for the evening. Later there's dessert, informal farewells, and we go our separate ways.

Tonight was no different. Freddie didn't make an appearance, which, while making me appear more informed to the rest of the table than I really was, also came as a disappointment to me. This was in part because I do look forward to guessing what new vampire movie he caught the previous week, but mainly because Jacob, through wit or treachery, somehow managed to come out on top in our debate over my employment.

Apparently, I'll be applying for work at his office over the weekend, but it's really just a formality. He tells me they'll have me on the payroll by Monday so long as I don't do anything stupid, such as being myself.

# CHAPTER THREE

## APRIL 29TH

Fortune favors the bold.

At least, that's what they say.

But they don't know a thing about dysfunctional vampire sibling rivalry.

As for me, whether wise or not, the sentiment was one I wholly intended to ignore by slinking into Barlowe's well over an hour late.

It wasn't that I hadn't been looking forward to the evening, the bad food, or the unconventionally furry staff; it was the company that concerned me.

In particular, it was Jacob.

He was livid.

And the subject of his anger?

Yours truly.

Things had gone perfectly over the weekend: I showed up for the interview on time and dressed to spec, played the part of an overpaid technology professional looking for a change of pace, was hired on the spot and told to show up at eight a.m. sharp Monday morning, a feat I somehow managed to pull off without injuring myself.

All things considered, not a bad start.

But it was all downhill from there. My overly developed sense of danger picked up on that the moment I walked through the front door.

For starters, the office had something of a strict dress code. I've never had the pleasure of observing one, but apparently they frown upon pretty much everything in my wardrobe. In the case of my Monday attire, it was an old shirt, khaki shorts, and a pair of beat-up sneakers.

Then there was the overall lack of humor. In my old job, pranks were the norm, showing up in someone's coffee, on the seat of a chair, or perched over a closed door almost daily, and you could be sure your next encounter with the business end of a practical joke was never far off. Not true at the firm, where several attempts on my part served both to annoy my new coworkers and new boss alike.

But none of this compared to my supreme blunder of the day, which – as the esteemed lawmaker Murphy could have seen coming from a mile off – would have been nothing to write home about if it didn't involve the bathroom.

No one had mentioned to me that the firm's formal restrooms were for visiting clientele only, and while their palatial stalls, piped-in melodies, and gold-printed toilet paper were a delight for the senses, those of us working in the trenches were condemned to using little more than a janitorial closet a floor down and out of sight. It wasn't much more than a hole in the wall, one whose primary residents were of the eight-legged variety, and if you're one of the many who believe vampires are impervious to arachnophobia, you haven't met many.

But I was quite oblivious to bathroom protocol during my first venture of the day, and while normally such use of the amenities would have constituted little more than a minor infraction, as it turned out the facility I chose wasn't up to the task of dealing with the danger skirting around in my digestive tract.

It was a disaster in the making, and after the ensuing overflow escaped into the general office area, the maintenance crew flew into action, closing the room for emergency repairs, a desperate act that would subject over a dozen different potential clients to the horrors of the janitor's closet.

And that was just Monday.

The rest of the week was better, but Jacob's image was already tarnished, and in the days to follow I found myself avoiding him as best I could, a task made rather impossible by the fact that he apparently suffers from severe deficiencies in the technology department.

Now, if you've ever handheld your grouchy lawyer vampire brother through the task of connecting a temperamental cell phone to a moody mail system, then you can likely relate to what I was going through. If you haven't, then stop what you're doing, fold your hands, close your eyes, and say a big Thank You to God Almighty.

The point is, while evasion was a tactic I could scarcely employ at the firm, what with the issue of proximity to the subject of my avoidance and the ongoing attention his hopeless ineptitude required of my services, it was most certain to fail at Barlowe's.

Turns out, it wasn't necessary.

When I arrived, Jacob was nowhere to be seen.

The others were present, though, Annie and Larry whispering tactfully as he loomed over the table like a hunchback giant, pen and notepad at the ready for the order he would inevitably oblige us to accept, and Freddie leaning back into his seat with hands folded, a look of apathetic disdain in his eyes, his open trench coat and button-down shirt doing little to hide his upper-chest, and his hair an explosion of orange curls.

There was something familiar about his appearance, but I must admit he had me perplexed from the moment I saw him – his was not the guise of any vampire I could recall.

He rolled his eyes in my direction as I approached, though the look on his face failed to change. "Hey, Freddie," I broke the ice. "What's new, other than the mop?"

His pupils ascended as if to take in the disheveled object of my remark, then returned their stare upon me. "Your employment, I hear," he replied, his monotone voice strangely slow-paced as he looked me over, suddenly intrigued. "Some excellent attire you've graced us with tonight."

I glanced down at myself, only then realizing I'd never arrived for dinner dressed quite as formally as I was just then: shirt, tie and all. "Yeah, well," I answered, taking my seat, "My first paycheck will be going to pay for it. If I last that long, anyway."

"Why wouldn't you last?"

The inquiry caught me off guard. Not that it wasn't a perfectly legitimate question, but from Freddie, well, it just wasn't the sort of thing he'd ask. He rarely took much interest in our affairs, least of all from the moment our traditionally one-sided dialogues began.

"If I had to pick just one reason," I answered, "I'd say it's the suits. You know, they've got no sense of humor at all. A bunch of stiffs, if you ask me."

"Now that's something."

"What?"

"A vampire calling a lawyer a stiff."

I stared at him a moment, amusement hidden behind his face. "Who are you supposed to be again?"

He waved the question away with dramatic flair. "Merely a loyal patron of this truly superb but otherwise unknown culinary establishment forgotten in the heart of a city all grown up from the small town of its youth and blah blah blah ad nauseam."

I hardly knew where to start with that, so I tackled the most obvious fiction to be found in the claim. "Superb? Freddie, the food's second-rate, overpriced, and shows up at the table with unwelcome side orders of fur. There's nothing superb about it."

"Your mouth says no, but your belly says yes."

I examined his appearance once more, trying to work out his persona, but coming up empty once again, I decided to let it go for now and focus on more pressing needs.

Like Annie and Larry, still whispering together and within reach of a good slap.

For a moment, I considered it, but resigned myself to a dirty look instead.

Not that I ever recommend slapping a werewolf.

Or a vampire, for that matter.

Or a female vampire who happens to be a cop.

Or a male werewolf with a romantic interest in said female vampire, who also happens to be your waiter.

In fact, as a general rule, keep your hands completely to yourself when dealing with any one or combination of the above.

Freddie must have seen the look I was sending their way because he turned to them and interrupted their discourse with a loud, sarcastic whine. "If you two don't mind, it's rarely considered polite for the hired help to converse in front of the clientele."

Whatever they were discussing, the comment kicked it squarely in the rear end, leaving Larry looking surprised and Annie hanging on whatever he certainly wasn't about to say in front of us now. But after a moment they found their composure, Larry rising and closing his notebook and Annie slumping back into her seat. "Sorry," she apologized. "We were just discussing the case."

"Really." Freddie didn't seem surprised at all. I think it was more sarcasm, but I couldn't be sure as I found myself again preoccupied with the elusive character of his appearance. He continued. "Would that be the case concerning the murders on the street as of late?"

"You mean the maulings that have been all over the news?"

"I mean the murders."

She started at him quizzically. "Are we talking about the same thing?"

He leaned back, folding his hands, but his eyes never left hers. "I find your choice of words rather telling."

"What choice of words? What are you talking about?" Clearly she was quite lost now.

She wasn't alone.

"What I mean is, while they're all murders, you insist on calling them maulings. In fact, I can't remember you referring to them any other way since the bodies started showing up."

"He's got a point," I jabbed, not really knowing what it was.

"And what's that?" Annie asked. "And how would you know what's on the news, anyway? Last I checked, you only watched the channels you had to pay for."

Freddie continued. "A murder insinuates a typical human killing. A mauling insinuates..." and he raised his eyebrows in my direction.

"A werewolf killing," I finished his thought.

"Precisely."

Annie shook her head. "But Larry insists the lycans aren't involved."

"Then why do you persist on treating this investigation as if they are?"

Okay, so he had a point after all.

A good point, actually.

I don't know if it had any merit, but there was no denying that Annie had only ever referred to the murders with the implications of lycan butchery.

But Annie wasn't one to let anyone question her motives to her face, and I could feel the tension in her voice as she answered. "Because werewolf or not, someone is slaughtering innocent people, and that's a mauling in my book any way you cut it."

"To you, maybe, but not to the media and not to the public, and you of all people should know that. Tell me, does the entire force share your enthusiasm for suggestive homicidal terminology?"

"That's enough, Frederick," a voice of authority ruptured the growing discord, and I had only a fleeting moment of blissful ignorance before my neurons delivered the bad news to the region of my brain most concerned with self-preservation – it was Jacob.

He approached from across the room, slapping shut his cell hard and shoving it into his front pocket as he bore down upon our table. I don't know what had been so important that it was worth him letting his coffee fend for itself, but it hardly mattered as he took his seat, sparing me only half a glare before returning his attention to Freddie.

"You know what Father would do to you if he heard you talking to your sister that way?"

Freddie yawned, letting his stare wander away from the table, ignoring the question.

Jacob's eyes grew narrow. "Are you listening to me, *Leech*?"

Leech was an old nickname of Freddie's, one that had fallen out of habit long after it fell out of favor. No one called him that anymore unless they meant to drive home a point.

Surprisingly, it was enough. Freddie's face cringed, and for a moment he wasn't just another eccentric vampire role model. He was our younger brother again.

But if there's one thing I've learned about brothers, young and old, it's that they're surprisingly quick to recover from authority – and to turn on you when you least expect it.

Respectively, that is.

So when Freddie retorted, I should have known Jacob would take out his irritation on me.

Freddie rolled his eyes once more, then replied "It's been said that when the law is against you, argue the facts. When the facts are against you, argue the law. And when both are against you, call the other lawyer names. I thought your standards were higher than this."

"My standards have been slipping, especially when it comes to this family. Doubly so concerning your brother."

"I'm right here, you know," I raised my hand with a cocked grin.

"Are you? I didn't recognize you without your usual shoddy apparel."

"Jacob!" Annie scolded him. "What's with you tonight?"

He dropped his head, rubbing his eyes with both hands. "Sorry, sorry," he mumbled. "It's been a long week, and there have been a lot of problems at work. Not *all* of which," he added, glancing at me, "were your fault."

That meant a lot coming from him. I wondered if he really meant it.

Ah, better to assume he did or fell and hit his head on his way in. I really didn't have a preference; either option brought a smile to my face.

"It's this trial we're working on," he continued. "We go to court in less than a week and the mayor's stonewalling our attempts to get key information released for the prosecution. That's what the call was about: another of his lackeys 'lost' a vital piece of evidence just hours before he was due to turn it over." He sighed. "Fifty bucks says

Blackburg's got ties to every contractor in the city. The guy's got more corruption than an Illinois governor."

"They're about due for a replacement," I joked. "I think the current gov's dishonesty has just about run out, so it *must* be time to vote another one in. Might as well be Blackburg."

That actually got a smile out of him.

Score one for the comic.

"Still," he straightened up, turning his attention back to Freddie, "You shouldn't talk to your sister like that. She's been knee-deep in this investigation since day one, and the last thing she needs is a lecture from you. Although," and now his eyes found their way to Annie, "you *have* referred to these murders as maulings since the case was opened. In fact, we all have. Now, think about that for a moment. Is there any chance this is just a coincidence?"

She opened her mouth to reply, then changed her mind, sitting back and growing thoughtful. "When the first bodies were discovered, we were certain the victims were killed by lycans. But as the investigation proceeded, some of the men assigned to the case began to question that assumption. And after Larry donated some of his hair for testing last week, forensics determined that the fur found in the wounds of the dead was not werewolf fur after all."

"Really?" Jacob asked. "What was it, then?"

"Wolf fur."

"Just as I suspected," Larry's deep voice reminded us all that he had never left.

Jacob leaned back, looking up at him. "Really."

Larry nodded. "As I said before, werewolves aren't involved in these murders. The killings are merely meant to look as if they are. *This* evidence supports that."

"So what?" Freddie spoke up once more, his voice regaining some of its former sarcasm, though it had lost its edge. "So the murderer isn't a lycan. The killer is still on the loose, the police still have no suspects, and the public's faith in the law's ability to put an end to it all is still in decline. Listening to the rest of you go on, I was beginning to think we were building up to some sort of happy ending."

Jacob tapped his chin in thought. "True that this evidence suggests that Larry is correct, but while the murders may have been staged to appear lycanthrope in design, that does not preclude the possibility that lycans *are* involved."

"I don't understand," Larry's omnipresent voice spoke down from above.

"Neither do I," Annie replied.

I've had lines stolen out of my mouth before, but never twice and by two different people just as I was clearing my throat. I suppose I should be glad they saved me the trouble.

Jacob continued. "What better way to sidestep suspicion than by framing yourself with a frame any dimwit could see through?"

"*You* didn't see through it," Larry answered, now slightly annoyed.

"I'm a lawyer, not a detective. Given enough time, even the police would have figured out the fur they found was not of lycan origin."

"So now you're suggesting werewolves are involved after all?" Annie asked.

Jacob waited a moment, lifting his coffee cup to within an inch of his lips, considering his answer. "No." As expected, followed by a long slurp.

"Okay," I said, throwing up my arms. "I'm officially lost. *Again.* Anyone have a map handy?"

"I confess I am lost as well," Freddie contributed his own opinion. "Jacob, do you think the rest of civilized society hates lawyers because they run around shutting down little girls' lemonade stands and suing waiters for sneezing in coffee pots?"

Larry coughed uncomfortably.

Jacob gave a suspicious glance into his cup, held between mouth and table, but gave no reply. Freddie continued.

"They're hated because they're so full of their own crap they can hardly make a simple point without wearing a diaper." He sent an apprehensive glance in the direction of Jacob's pants. "I hope for our sake you've got at least two on."

"I'm simply trying to think outside the box here," Jacob replied, setting his cup down with a hard ring. "I don't know if the lycans are behind the murders or not. Perhaps the murderers are vampires. Perhaps they're human. They could be neurotic undead monkeys who only come out at night and have a tragic sense of the ironic. My point is that we cannot afford to rule anything out just because of a single piece of evidence."

"Perhaps they're monkeys who *look* like werewolves," I offered up.

"Or werewolves in sheep's clothing," Freddie added.

"Or maybe they're lawyers with no social lives who thrive on dysfunction and pointless conflict," Larry offered up.

"Well, I think our friend here may be on to something," Freddie replied with a smile. "Annie, I hope you're taking notes."

"I'm finished!" Jacob threw down his napkin in disgust. "Goodnight."

And with that, he rose from his chair and stormed out.

"There goes one socially inept lawyer," Freddie muttered after he'd left, then turned to Annie. "I do hope you break the case soon. I don't think our Thursday nights can take much more of this."

## ∾Ι NTERLUDE∾

The Blood Laws were passed when I was just a child. Back then vampires were still second-class citizens, not unlike the men and women of the civil rights movements of the mid-twentieth century, only this second-class habitually killed and drank the blood of the first.

Sure, vampires have always been around, but since day one we've been in the minority. And unlike werewolves, whose main character flaw comes out just once a month and can be controlled with the proper precautions (not unlike a certain character flaw in another species you may know), and zombies, who have really always been more of a nuisance than anything, vampires will forever be a race whose survival depends upon the blood of others. With that blood being something of a necessity to those whose bodies produce it naturally, you can see how common sense frowns upon the possibility of coexistence with anyone possessing even the slightest inkling of self-preservation.

But somewhere along the line, it became obvious that anything short of a complete genocide of the vampire people would do little to resolve the stalemate between the races. And despite their advantage in numbers, humans have never been willing to risk a war against us.

After all, what if they lost?

The Blood Laws were a compromise.

In short, they require every healthy human over the age of eighteen to donate a moderate amount of blood to their local blood bank on a regular basis. This blood, once processed, becomes the core ingredient of our medicine, ensuring that no vampire need kill to survive.

Not that there haven't been murders on both sides since the laws were enacted. One must expect the occasional rogue vampire to succumb to his primal instincts and take a life for the thrilling consumption of raw, unrefined blood, and there will always be humans who refuse to live alongside even cultured vampires.

But for most, the arrangement has worked, and while the laws haven't bought us complete peace and equality, they have carried us as close to harmonious existence as I think we can ever hope to achieve in a civilized society.

Now, as I said, when the laws were passed I was young, just a few years old. Jacob and Annie were seven and five, respectively, and Mother was still pregnant with Freddie.

But unlike her previous births, which she carried out with minimal complications, this pregnancy was difficult for her. She was always sick, she gained little weight, and to further complicate matters, blood was in scarce supply. Back then there were no blood banks, and it was both difficult and dangerous for any vampire to obtain sustenance.

Father insisted she drink, and for a time we received cartons of unrefined fluid delivered under cover of night to the back door, always by shadowy figures without faces or names. Father claimed the blood came from an old friend overseas, but even then we knew better. Years later, when I first heard of the Black Market, it started to make sense.

But then something happened that even Father could never have predicted.

Mother found religion.

Well, it wasn't *quite* that simple. First, her sister died. Then, she fell into depression. Depression led to isolation, isolation to reflection, and reflection to a newfound conviction in the existence of something greater.

A conviction only compounded by her weakening state.

But my problem with religion and the very reason vampires in general tend to avoid it is that aside from the occasional pagan off-shoot, it rarely approves of the consumption of blood.

And therein lies the dilemma in which my mother found herself.

Not to overstate the obvious, but a vampire who willingly chooses to give up blood is unusual to say the least, mainly because it eventually leads to an untimely and exceedingly unpleasant death. But for Mother, it was a sacrifice she was willing to make for the sake of her newfound principles. And besides, with the laws and the politicians barking their nonsense about change for the future, she believed that soon she'd have no need of raw blood anyway.

Perhaps she thought she could outlast the slow pace of the bureaucratic engine.

Perhaps she knew she wouldn't.

But to those familiar, politics is nothing if not a hornet's nest of red tape, and it would take years for the blood banks and the pills and the distribution of medicine to establish itself as a normal part of everyday life. And while she waited, Mother withered away.

At first Father insisted she drink human blood to maintain her health, but when it became clear she would not have it, he began to push animal blood in its place. But that, too, somehow violated her beliefs, and so he resorted to slipping small measures into her drinks and even her meals. But she got wise to that as well: he wasn't much of a chef. She prepared all her own meals anyway, making the whole undertaking much more difficult, and she had a nose for when something wasn't right, besides.

She gave birth at last, but she didn't last long after that; her body was simply too weak to sustain her after the trauma. Her funeral was held in Northgate Cemetery on a dreary fall afternoon, with only a few of us in attendance. Freddie was barely a month old. I still remember

Father carrying him from the gravesite, a cold, uncaring look in his eyes.

It must have been hard on him. For us, too young to understand the loss, life went on. And while we grew up, Father grew distant.

Freddie grew too, but it soon became obvious that something wasn't right. He was slow, a late bloomer, his teachers said, though they were always quick to add that he was sure to come around sooner or later – all children eventually did. But not Freddie, and by the time the school system quietly ushered him into the fourth grade with hardly a whisper, he was already behind by three.

Father did what he could, and you never saw a child consume so many glasses of plasma, but the damage was already done. Freddie simply hadn't gotten the necessary nutrients from Mother while she was pregnant, and he would live with the consequences for the rest of his life.

That's why he is the way he is now – or at least, that's why we think he's that way. I suppose it could just be his personality, but he's always been so different that none of us really believe it.

A lot had happened since our last meal together.

Things had gotten better at work. Sometime over the weekend Jacob must have either forgiven me or forgotten about me, and on Monday things were more or less back to normal: no dress code blunders, no plumbing mishaps, no pranks gone awry.

In fact, the only real issue I ran into at the firm was a widespread system outage which, while initially blamed on me for being in the wrong place at the wrong time, was eventually traced to a problem which had been present and reported to upper management some time ago, before being promptly ignored.

But that's life in IT – everyone's an expert until something goes horribly wrong, at which point the techs are forced to become heroes to fix it while being treated like villains for failing to prevent it, and all of it despite the overpaid, under-achieving idiot of a VP who failed to heed warnings by email, voice mail, and in person, delivered by those very same techs.

Jacob's team of lawyers had finally obtained all but a few pieces of evidence needed to establish a firm prosecution for their case. They went to court on Monday appearing confident, and they came back shaking each other's hands and looking abundantly pleased with themselves. With no slamming of doors or grumbling of oral cavities, I took it all as a good sign.

The week had been good to Annie, as well. The police had made a number of arrests and had several suspects in custody whom they believed to be connected to the murders. I thought to myself while catching a rare glimpse of news that even if the suspects didn't pan out, at least the media had something positive to report about the force for a change, and that should make my sister smile no matter what.

But the police weren't releasing any real information just yet, and as a result, I found myself looking forward to Barlowe's more than usual as I plodded through the week. I was certain that whatever had been uncovered would be shared and picked apart over our meal.

And yet, as surely as I was anticipating the news, as much as I was looking forward to another round of semi-intellectual debates with Jacob, as truly ready as my stomach was for a plate full of Mister Barlowe's world-famous steak and eggs, it was Freddie who once again monopolized my every sense as I entered.

Now, I'll admit I returned home after our last meal together more or less lost concerning his guise of the evening. Of course I didn't admit it, or ask Annie or Jacob, assuming they had either figured it out already or didn't care enough to waste their time. But my curiosity kept growing as it finds itself compelled always to do when something completely insignificant and ultimately pointless crosses my path.

On a related note, it's truly amazing how many of the critical functions of my life take a backseat to unimportant peculiarities.

But while Freddie's masquerade of the previous week had offered up nothing if not dry humor and an overabundance of sarcasm, this week I knew even before taking my seat that his personality would ensure our night be one filled with temperamental angst, melodramatic pouting, and an ample supply of poor acting.

And all that would be just fine, so long as Larry kept his shirt on.

"I can't believe you finally did it," I joked as I got comfortable.

"What are you talking about?" he asked, his voice unusually pained, a detail I barely noticed as I took in the tower of gelled hair rising precariously over his shamelessly white forehead, a look he somehow managed to pull off with greater absurdity than his mangled orange curls of the week before.

"You know *exactly* what I'm talking about," I answered him.

"Despite what you may be thinking, I cannot read your mind."

"There, you see? You've got the look *and* the attitude." I couldn't help but grin. "I'm going to enjoy this."

"Then I hope you enjoy disappointment."

"I'm a comedian working in an office full of lawyers. I'd say I enjoy it well enough."

He gave me a tormented look, then opened his mouth to answer, but couldn't bring himself to speak, struggling against what appeared to be tears that wouldn't come.

For a moment I wasn't entirely sure if this was part of the act or not, but then another detail caught my eye. "Is that lipstick you're wearing?"

His angst was replaced by a look of perplexity, and his brow furrowed, an amazing feat considering its unusual height. And what was that on his skin?

Powder?

*Glitter?*

"I hope you realize," I went on, "that not only is this your worst attempt ever at choosing a vampire to idolize, it's also, *by far*, the single most —"

"Gayton can suck it!" Annie barked triumphantly as she entered our section, swinging a newspaper and slapping it down on the table as she took both her seat and the final word from out of my mouth.

"Gayton?" I asked, only a little surprised at the timely coincidence.

"Gayton," she repeated, as if I'd insulted her by not knowing. "*Detective* Gayton." She pointed to the front page of the paper. I picked it up and scanned the headlines. The banner wasn't doing its part to help, shouting only "Midnight Mauler in Custody?"

I let the unhelpful informant drop. "The Midnight Mauler?"

She ignored me. "Gayton's been taking point on the case since it first opened. He's also the idiot responsible for the constant leaks to the press, not to mention over half a dozen failed theories on what's really going on. But not anymore."

"What do you mean?"

"I've been trying for a while now to get the chief to back me on a surveillance mission. He's been resisting, what with all the extra manpower required, but he finally bought into it. I don't think he really believed it would pan out, but he's been under a lot of pressure from the mayor to produce results, and if nothing else, a large-scale sting would show the public we're doing more than chasing clues and wrapping bodies."

"And did it? Pan out, I mean."

"We've got four suspects in custody. I'd say it was a success." She leaned back and folded her arms. "Not to mention it finally convinced the chief to kick Gayton off the case completely."

"So who's in charge now?"

"You're looking at her."

I blinked. "Really?"

"Really," she tipped her head.

I studied her a moment. She seemed a fair bit more pleased with herself than usual. In fact, she seemed a fair bit more pleased with herself than I'd seen her in a long time.

But then, why not? The case was moving forward and she'd been bumped up the department ladder. It sounded like things were finally going her way.

Still, one thing bothered me. "The Midnight Mauler? *Really?*"

She rolled her eyes. "You know the press."

Actually, I didn't. A bunch of dirt-digging vultures if you ask me, and quite possibly the only group of people worse than lawyers. I have a theory that law school is what happens to reporters who aren't any good at their job, and reporting is what happens to lawyers who are.

It's all about failing upwards.

"I'd have taken a shot at it," I answered her.

"Indulge me."

I thought about it a moment, then gave her my best. "The Back Street Stabber."

She snorted. "That's awful. Besides, he doesn't stab – he mauls. If he's a he at all."

"He *murders*," Freddie corrected. We both looked at him, his expression as wounded as ever. "No blood, no foul, you know."

"Thanks, Fredward," I replied. Then, to my sister, "Okay, so the Midnight Murderer is more accurate, but it still sucks. And what do you mean, if he's a he?"

"How do you know he's not a she?"

"I don't. But that changes things."

"How so?"

"We wouldn't have a Midnight Murderer on our hands. We'd have a Midnight Murder*ess*."

"You're kidding."

"Look it up." In truth, I really rather hoped she wouldn't. I generally don't have nearly as much faith in my claims as I try to portray.

That probably doesn't speak very highly of me.

"He's right," Jacob chimed in. His comment surprised me as much as his presence, which I had somehow managed to overlook until just then, although his latest book, a gigantic tome held wide between his face and the rest of the table, may have been just the distraction my subconscious required to convince the rest of my brain he was absent.

"*Really?*" Annie and I both asked him in unison.

The word seemed to be coming up more often than usual this evening.

"So the papers," Jacob continued, glasses and nose poking out over the top of the bind, "seem to think that not only do the police have the murderer in custody, but also that he is, in fact, a he."

"Oh, don't start again," Annie dropped her face into her hands, peering back at him through her fingers. "I'm in too good a mood tonight for you to start reading between the lines of every little detail."

Jacob smiled, satisfied. "Very well. I'll just resign myself to my coffee, then, shall I?"

"You shall," I replied, then asked Annie "So *are* any of the suspects women?"

She gave me a dirty look.

"Oh, come on! I've been waiting all week to hear this. You've got to tell me what you know."

She sighed, then answered with a roll of her eyes. "We have four suspects in custody. They're all men. We don't know yet if any is the murderer."

Her reply was terse. Just the facts. Nothing more.

"How did you find them?" I pressed, hoping for more than the stale data she'd rattled off as if she'd rehearsed it a thousand times already.

"Loitering around where they didn't belong: in back alleys and such. Each was armed with a knife or another weapon capable of cutting flesh. Each has a record. None could provide an explanation."

"An explanation for what?"

Another dirty look from Annie – the forecast indicated more were to come – although the current stare seemed less to portray annoyance than to show surprise at just how idiotic I must have been to have missed the obvious. "*Why* they were loitering. *What* they were doing there. *Why* they were armed. *Those* explanations."

"You spoke of a demographic," Jacob interrupted her sarcastic rant. "A few weeks ago. 'Older individuals. Men and women both. Rich. Recently divorced or married. All humans.'"

That's the thing about Jacob. He's got a photographic memory.

Except when it comes to paying his share of the bill.

Or admitting he's wrong.

Or admitting that leaving without paying his share of the bill was wrong.

Come to think of it, there are quite a number of enigmas seemingly impervious to his otherwise perfect recollection, most of them concerning money owed or anything involving his many deficiencies as a person, but apparently nothing at all when it comes to the ramblings or character flaws of his siblings.

"Is that still the case?" Jacob asked.

"Yes," Annie replied. "Why?"

"Have you been able to make anything of it yet?"

She shook her head.

"What about the Marx?" Freddie muttered more than asked, his injured stare now drifting somewhere through the rafters above.

"The Marx Casino?" I asked. "Why do you say that?"

"Well," he answered, his gaze suddenly shifting across the table to the other side of the room, his face and hair trailing his eyes as if for dramatic effect. "If *I* wanted to rob someone, I'd look for someone older, someone who couldn't fight back. Someone with money to burn. Someone human." He paused, growing thoughtful. "Humans can't smell blood. Especially their own." He regained his usual composure for just a moment, suddenly realizing we were all staring, then added, "Not that I've ever thought about it."

"The Marx gets plenty of newlyweds," Jacob replied, setting his book down and removing his glasses. "And a fair number of divorcees, I'd imagine. People on Cloud Nine or on the fast track to the gutter."

"The Blackjack Burglar," I mused.

"He's not breaking into homes," Annie shot back, "He's *killing* people." Then she addressed us all. "These are murders for the sake of murder. Nothing is missing from the bodies when we get there."

"Nothing?" Larry's baritone voice rumbled across the table. I glanced over my shoulder, then the other, wondering if anyone else was hiding in plain sight, waiting to join in at just the right moment.

"Nothing," Annie replied with a cock of her head.

"How do you know?"

"Well, where should I start? Each victim has been found dressed in formal attire, the men in suits and the women in gowns, some of them in furs. Each has been found with a wallet or purse filled with cash, credit cards, and identification. The women are still wearing their jewelry. The men have their handkerchiefs and the women their makeup kits. They even have pocket change. There's nothing else."

Larry leaned down, putting away his notepad in his usual manner and placing his large hands on the edge of the table. It groaned, straining to support his muscular weight. He eyed her closely, then spelled it out for her, slower this time. "How. Do. You. Know?"

She sat back and folded her arms, tightening her lips but keeping quiet.

"It's a fair question," Jacob added, sipping beneath a doubtful stare he sent in Annie's direction. "Perhaps you're right; perhaps nothing's been taken. But perhaps something has. Something that's missing before you arrive. Something that links them all together."

She shook her head, clearly growing impatient now. "There have been nineteen murders over the past three months. What could possibly connect that many people?"

"You're the lead investigator," Jacob answered, shrugging. "You work it out."

I perked up. The tone in Jacob's voice – I'd heard it before. "You have a theory," I said.

He shook his head. "Nothing certain. But if Annie is correct, and these are murders for the sake of murder, then why is there a demographic at all? Two or three victims and it might be a coincidence. But nineteen? It doesn't make any sense."

Annie grew thoughtful. "Like I said, we haven't been able to determine the reason for the demographic."

"You have *established* one. For the moment that's all that matters. Come on, Annie, you're the one who's been pounding pavement for the past month! For crying out loud, Larry's just our waiter and he's worked it out!"

That got her attention.

In fact, it got all our attention, and at once all our faces were turned toward Larry, once again standing beside the table like a monolith of muscle, and now looking as shocked as the rest of us.

"Me?"

Jacob gestured up at him. "Yes, and you know it. There's a lot more going on in that furry mug of yours than you'll admit."

Larry's surprise faded, whisked away by intrigue. "You think so?" Jacob nodded. "Please. You've dropped so many hints over the past few weeks I'm surprised you're not tripping over them. In fact, I'd wager you've been waiting for someone to speak up." He glanced about. "What, hasn't anyone else noticed?" But his inquiring gaze was met only with professional interest, clueless bewilderment, and the melancholic grief of the eternally pubescent vampire.

"Fine," he snorted. "Since I seem to be the only one here paying any attention at all, I'll do you all a favor and point out the obvious." He raised his eyes to the hired help once more and extended a single finger. "Your notepad."

"My order pad?" Still surprised. "You mean the one I use to write down your dinner and drink selections? Yes, I can see how keeping it around is very unusual."

"Yes, yes, you're always jotting away in it, but never when we're ordering. Besides, you know all our orders by heart. In fact, you practically tell us what we want week after week. So what are you writing?"

Now, I don't know what went through the minds of the others when Jacob asked the question, but in that moment I experienced something I'd never known before, and quite likely never will again.

I think it was admiration.

Because Jacob was right.

Not only was he right, the rest of us must have been blind not to see it ourselves.

Larry stared him down, his face hard, but then the curl of a sly smile appeared upon the corner of his mouth. "You've a keen eye, my lawyer friend."

"Thank you. And two, just for the record."

Larry took a quick look around the dining room, then made an abrupt grab for a nearby chair, swinging it around backwards and dropping into it, facing us head on, his backside situated squarely upon its two arms. I made the passing observation that the seat had no hope of accommodating his girth the other way around.

Larry continued, his eyes upon Jacob. "You also have the ability to correctly analyze what you observe. Critical traits if one is to succeed in your line of work." He paused. "I do have a few thoughts, as a matter of fact."

Jacob opened his arms in welcome invitation. "Then by all means, indulge us."

Larry took a breath, then pulled out his notepad, flipped through a few pages, then began running his finger down a sheet that he kept from all eyes but his own. "Despite any claims to the contrary, the police have no motive, no suspects other than the four already in custody, and no idea yet if those are involved or not. There is no timetable for the murders – a body turns up one week, three more the week after that – although all have been found in the early morning. And there is no true geographic hub; the victims have turned up all over the city."

He looked at Annie. "On the other hand, what do the police have? A basic demographic: older men and women, all of them wealthy, all of them newly married or recently divorced. Am I getting this right so far?"

Annie, still dumbfounded by his unexpected insight, only nodded back.

He continued. "Now if I were the lead investigator probing these murders, my next step would be clear: to stake out the most obvious place from which each victim was returning when he or she was assaulted."

"Well, that's a *fantastic* plan," Annie answered, "But how are we supposed to know where they were before they were killed? For that matter, how do you know they were on their way home at all and not on their way out for the evening?"

Larry took a deep breath. A very deep breath. And with it, I could have sworn the hair on the back of his neck stood up. I'm really not sure what lycans look like when they grow impatient, but I think I was witnessing the first symptom right then.

I hoped for all our sakes I wouldn't have to see the second.

"As Jacob can no doubt tell you, murder sprees rarely follow haphazard rules. There is *always* an underlying order — a method to the madness, as it were. In this case, each body has been found the morning after the crime was committed; therefore, we can assume the killings take place late at night and not in the early evening. I assume your autopsies corroborate this?"

Annie nodded. "Sometime between eleven o'clock at night and one in the morning."

"All of them?"

"All of them."

"Very well. Not what I'd call conclusive evidence, but this does suggest they were not on their way out for the evening. In any case, their personal effects as found on their persons when their bodies were discovered may shed some additional light."

He looked the table over, then helped himself to the nearest glass of water, which as luck would have it was mine, and which as luck would have it I had not yet given up on just yet. I'd have called for another, but our waiter was preoccupied with licking his lips. Without so much as a thank you, he returned the glass to its former place and cleared his throat.

"As for knowing which items are missing, well, that's tricky. It's the chicken-and-the-egg: without knowing where they were, it's impossible to know what to look for and vice-versa. But there is one clue to be had here, or rather, one which isn't to be had, one which I find most puzzling, and one which I believe you have all overlooked."

That did it as far as piquing interest was concerned. A drum roll couldn't have cued up our anticipation better.

So while I'm not sure what my own face looked like just then, Annie stared back, breathless, while Jacob sat frozen, his cup held aloft, and Freddie held back another tear, his emotionally ravaged face bending under the weight of untold sorrow.

And that must have been enough for Larry, who relinquished his secret with a single phrase. "Their keys."

It was a revelation somewhat lost on this crowd, a feeling with which I am adequately familiar, as my own jokes tend to provoke the same response.

"Their keys," Annie repeated.

Larry nodded.

"What about them?" I asked.

"To begin with, where are they?"

"Maybe they lost them."

"All of them? Every single victim?"

I shrugged. "No one ever claimed murder victims had to be bright."

"Further, why would anyone with half a wit choose to walk these city streets at midnight while wearing jewelry and carrying pockets of cash? Why not drive?"

"Maybe they had too much to drink."

"Then why not call a taxi?"

"Maybe they had too much to drink," I repeated.

Larry smirked. "Annie?"

"Each of the victims was found with substantial alcohol in their systems."

"Above the legal limit?"

"Well above the limit," she answered.

"More likely, someone arranged a ride for them."

"Then perhaps it wasn't a cab," Jacob mumbled to himself.

Larry smiled a knowing smile. "Would you mind?" he invited, gesturing across the table.

"Sure, I'll give it a go," Jacob answered, getting comfortable. *If I didn't know better, those two were actually getting along rather well.*

*I suppose it all comes down to common interests. In this case: murder.*

*Though just then I was wishing our waiter's attention was more focused on the subject of food, most notably the act of retrieving ours from the kitchen. No need to concern ourselves with the pleasantries of ordering; I'm sure Larry had our selections worked out by then anyway.*

"The way I see it," he began, "either the victims each took a taxi out for the night, or they drove themselves. In any case, they wouldn't have walked, not with the streets as dangerous as they are, and not with that sort of cash on hand. And even if they did have too much to drink, that doesn't explain how they ended up where they were when they were killed." He thought a moment. "Annie?"

She looked up but said nothing.

Jacob continued. "The police have the identifications of each of the victims, so their home addresses are known. So what would happen if you marked the location of each body on a map –"

"–and drew a straight line from their home address to the location of their body, then continued it on to establish a central point of origin?" she interrupted. Apparently, she knew where he was going with this.

That made one of us.

"I take it you already have," Jacob answered.

"Yes, and it told us nothing we didn't already know. As far as we can tell, the victims were found at completely random locations throughout the city. There is no central point."

"That's what I thought. So even if they were headed home when they were killed, they weren't *on their way* home when it happened."

Annie shook her head. "You've lost me."

"Someone drove each victim to his or her place of death, and if they did that, there must have been a purpose. And if I had to venture a guess, it would have been to throw a dash of chaos into the equation – make this whole spree appear more haphazard than it actually is. But in so doing we can now deduce that someone must have been involved – someone pulling the strings, so to speak."

"Deduce?" I chuckled. "Nice work, Sherlock. You've cracked the case. *Of course* someone was involved! It was the *murderer!*" I half expected him to pull out a giant magnifying glass and clay pipe.

But Jacob didn't budge, his mood rigid and unimpressed. He seemed strangely focused, more so than I think I'd ever seen him before. "These murders have been planned. Organized. Carefully orchestrated so as to suggest one group is responsible while also confounding the investigation by throwing off all sense of order. That can't be mere chance. And if chance can be ruled out, then even the smallest oddity must not. In this case, the absence of their keys. Or more to the point, their cars."

"Annie," Larry asked, "have the police checked to see if any of the victims owns a car or truck, and have you located the vehicles?"

She shook her head. "Standard procedure doesn't require that level of investigation."

"Well, after nineteen murders I'd hope the force would consider digging a little beyond standard procedure."

Another dirty look from my sister. At least this one wasn't directed at me.

"You know," Jacob spoke up once more, "There are only a few businesses in the city capable of legally withholding a car from its owner. And of those, there are fewer still who offer valet parking, which might explain the lack of keys on the victims' bodies."

"And only one which might send someone home with pockets of cash?" Larry asked with a grin.

"Only one," Jacob answered. All eyes turned toward him, and with that much attention at his beck and call, what else could he do but take a long, loud slurp of coffee, just to add to the suspense?

"It seems Freddie had it figured out all along," he said at last. "Annie, if I were you, I would immediately stake out the Marx Casino both inside and out. It's starting to sound like your victims may be casino patrons."

# CHAPTER FIVE

## MAY 13TH

"It's broken," Jacob slapped his phone down on the table between us.

"It's not broken, and I've already told you that six times," I replied, both our patience toward the matter having run out long ago.

But even without patience, Jacob still had perseverance to spare. "If it's not broken, then why won't it send emails? Why won't it *receive* emails? And why can't I get online?"

"Because your carrier suspended your account due to nonpayment, and I can't fix that. Only your accounting department can."

"I spoke to the head of the accounting department this afternoon. They paid the bill. And the phone still doesn't work."

"Then your accounting department's also broken. That's what you get for hiring an imp to pay the bills."

"The *phone* is what's broken! And he's not an imp; he's from overseas."

"It's not the phone. The phone is fine. It turns on. It gets a signal. It can call 911. It's *not* the phone."

"How do you know it can call 911?"

"*All* cells can call 911. Even without a service plan."

"That's not what I meant."

"You don't believe I tested it?"

Jacob grabbed for his coffee. "I haven't decided yet."

I sat back in my chair, irritated. If there's one thing I hate about working as a tech, it's the unwavering faith of the idiot user looking for the 'any' key that he knows my job better than I do. "Listen, Jake," I began, all pleasantries lost, "the lady who answered when I called was none too thrilled when I told her my emergency was an irate twelve o'clock flasher with a serious personality deficiency."

"So now it's my fault you lack both technical knowhow *and* people skills?"

"What are you two arguing about now?" Annie cut short our squabble as she collapsed into her chair, draping a light coat over the seatback as she got comfortable. Her arrival may have been uncommonly late, but it was far from lacking its usual interruption, and for once I was truly grateful for the disturbance. The dispute had by now long lost its enjoyable taste, having started back at the office that afternoon and then picking up all over again the moment we entered Barlowe's for the evening.

Jacob said nothing, looking away instead as he downed an unhealthy dose of coffee.

I turned to my sister to find her eyeing me with an inquiring stare and cocked head.

That was a look I knew well.

"What's going on?" she demanded more than asked.

"It's his phone," I replied, toning down my voice for the first time since I took my seat.

But that wasn't enough for inquiring minds. "What about it?"

"It's broken," Jacob spoke up.

"It's not broken," I insisted, my voice already rising.

"Oh, I see," Annie said, a smile crossing her face. "Sibling rivalry in the workplace finally rearing its ugly head? I warned you this was a bad idea."

"It's not rivalry," Jacob insisted. "It's a serious lack of expertise."

"You're right," I added. "When it comes to technology, you don't have any."

Jacob nodded toward his phone, still sitting face-up in the center of the table. "I'm not supposed to. You are. And if you did, my cell wouldn't be suffering right now, would it?"

"It's been suffering since the day you got it," I shot back, snatching it up from its place of unrest. Then, looking at Annie, I asked "Can I borrow yours for a sec?"

She stared back at me, as if unsure of what bleak fate awaited it should she hand it over. But her confidence in me must have prevailed, for she reached into her pocket and pulled it out, handing it carefully across the table. "Don't go poking around in there."

"I'm not going to break it, if that's what you mean."

"That's what I mean." Then she added "But there's also department data on there, which you *won't* look at. Understand?"

Out of the corner of my eye, I caught Jacob eyeing me with a curious stare, our disagreement momentarily lost. "I mean it!" Annie insisted.

"All right!" I laughed. "I'm not going to do anything with it. I just want to prove Jacob wrong, that's all."

"Indeed," Jacob spoke up, putting his cup down and folding his hands, his annoyance suddenly spent. "Prove me wrong. By the way, Annie, did you happen to park in the back lot tonight?"

She raised her eyebrows. "Yes. Why?"

He shrugged. "I think I heard someone mention they'd be flushing the hydrants out back this evening. You might want to make sure your windows are rolled up."

"Great," she blurted out, then rose, grabbing her jacket, and walked out. I gave Jacob a sideways look.

"How did you know her windows were open? It's not warm out." In fact, it had been unseasonably cold all week, feeling more like March than early May.

"She always leaves them open. She can't stand the smell of leather, so what do you suppose all the unmarked department vehicles come with? Leather interiors. Your tax dollars at work. Anyway, it makes her sick, so she leaves them cracked. She even puts plastic over the back seats and hangs air fresheners from the mirrors. Can you believe it?"

"What's wrong with air fresheners?" The Gremlin was no stranger to foul odors, even when I *wasn't* driving.

"Nothing, if you drive a car like yours, which unfortunately you do. Now," he eyed Annie's cell hungrily, "what do we have here?"

I grinned. A few keystrokes later and we were breaking our sister's one rule. Well, one of her two rules, anyway – I fully intended to return the phone to her in working order.

"Let's see…" I mumbled. "Emails, contacts, photos… Whoa." I blinked. "Who's she trying to impress?"

"Knock it off," he said, grabbing it out of my hands. "We've only got a minute before she gets back. Hmmm…" He tapped the keys like a madman, searching for anything worth digging up, like a modern-day pirate searching for gold in a silicon treasure chest.

"This is interesting," he said at last.

"What?"

"It looks like our sister's been emailing herself lab data over the past couple days. There's quite a lot in here on forensic solutions."

"Such as?"

"Sodium fluoride, potassium oxalate. Lots of references to silver nitrate." He grew suddenly quiet, and I found myself drawn to his face, his look one of deep concentration. "What is it?" I asked.

He squinted. "Larry's been emailing her, too."

"What?" I asked, grabbing the phone back, leaving him both surprised and annoyed. Sure enough, intermingled with the emails sent
to herself were numerous messages from our waiter. "Maybe he finally
got up the courage to break the ice," I commented. "He's had a thing
for her for a while now."

"Read the headings," Jacob said, simply.

I scanned the email titles, realizing at once that these messages
were of the professional type. "So maybe he's helping her out with the
investigation," I tried again.

"He *has* proven he's a lot smarter than he lets on," Jacob agreed.
"But still, doesn't that seem just a little strange to you?"

"What do you mean?" as I continued scrolling through the
correspondence.

"Annie's been trying to rise through the ranks for a while now.
How would it look if she broke her first big case with the help of a
waiter?"

I thought about that. "Maybe she's really that desperate."

"Maybe," he lifted his cup and took a slow sip.

"And maybe he's just the man for the job," I spoke up again. One
email in particular, dated three nights past, caught my eye, its title a
peculiar contrast to the rest. I held the phone up, screen facing Jacob
so he could read it for himself.

"I've Solved It," he read the title aloud. "Larry cracked the case?"

"I don't know," I replied, resuming my own examination of the
device. "All the message says is 'We have to talk.'"

"Did she reply?"

I scrolled through the messages once more. "Nope. In fact, that
was the last email he sent her. After that, there's nothing but the lab
data. Huh…"

"What?"

"You know, she didn't send herself *any* of this info until after Larry's last message."

"Strange.  Maybe one of them called the other.  Or maybe they spoke in person."

"Or maybe Larry's just jumping the gun and Annie's taking her time to verify the facts."

"Maybe," Jacob answered, his voice hushed.  "Here she comes.  Don't say anything, understand?  Let me handle this."

In no time at all, Annie was back at our side and looking rather annoyed as she sat between us.  "The back lot, Jacob?  There aren't even any hydrants out there."

Jacob did his best to hold back a smile.  "Did I say the back lot?  I meant the side."

She gave him a dirty look, then held out her hand to me.  "Can I have my phone back, please?"

I gave it back to her and she tucked it away, asking "Have either of you seen Larry?"

In reply, Jacob held up his cup and I lifted my first soda of the night, already half empty.

"Of course you have," Annie mumbled absent-mindedly, then added, "I'm parched."

"I'm sure he's around here somewhere," I smiled, "probably hanging around in back with the rest of the crime-fighting staff."

Jacob coughed.

Annie gave me a quizzical look.

"Well, maybe not crime-fighting," I continued.  "More like crime-*solving*."

Jacob coughed again, this time louder.  I wondered if this was a tactic he employed in front of the bench.

If it was, I hope it wasn't his best.

"Come on," I continued. "You can't tell me you weren't impressed with his surprise show of deduction last week."

"He caught me off guard, that's for sure." Annie conceded. "But a crime-solver he is not. Believe me."

"How do you know?" I asked, opening my arms in a show of endorsement. "I'll bet he could solve a case or two. In fact, I'll bet that given *enough* facts he might even be able to solve your own case. Who knows? Maybe he already has."

"I knew it," Annie answered back, slamming her hands down on the table, her voice sharp with anger. "I just *knew* it!"

Jacob cleared his throat. "Knew what, exactly?"

She glared at us, one at a time. "You looked through my emails."

I gave her my best innocent-and-genuinely-hurt look.

I'm fairly certain it failed on both counts.

"You two are a pair of real jerks, you know that?"

"That's rather –," I began, talking over Jacob's "I'm not sure –"

"Well, you are," she interrupted. "Both of you! LARRY!"

From out of nowhere he appeared, and I noticed he was being more generous than usual with our personal space, as if he was uncertain of our sister's striking distance.

Without waiting for him to offer his condolences on our swiftly-deteriorating evening, Annie barked her instructions. "Water. Now." As if the words weren't enough, she let her finger do its own talking on the surface of the table as she spoke.

He looked at her a moment, anxiety holding him in place, then turned and disappeared out of sight.

"You know, you don't *have* to be rude to him," Jacob commented. "I'm sure he's not holding out on you in the beverage department."

"Oh, so now you're defending him?" she demanded. "I thought you hated him."

He frowned thoughtfully. "To be honest, after last week I can't help but admire the man."

"What, his detective skills?"

"Not so much as his ability to hide them from us for so long."

That gave her something to think about. "I suppose. But don't go changing the subject. I'm mad at you, and I want to keep it that way."

He shrugged. "Fair enough. But now that the cat's out of the bag, what did he mean when he said he solved it?"

"Exactly what it sounds like."

"Wait," I spoke up. "Larry really did crack the case?"

Annie shook her head and rolled her eyes. "Not even close."

"What was his theory?"

She sighed. "It doesn't matter. I'll spare you the details for his sake." She paused, then gave us an uncertain glance. "You didn't look through my photos, did you?"

I looked at Jacob.

Jacob looked at me.

We both looked at Annie. "Photos?" I asked.

Annie leaned back, cradled her head in her hands. "Ohhh…" she sighed, shaking her head.

"So getting back to it," Jacob continued, "Whatever came of our discussion last week? Did you stake out the casino?"

She nodded, bouncing back to life and apparently forgetting all about being mad at us. "We did. And we checked the casino records for the past few months. And you were right: every victim was a patron."

"And did they drive there?" I asked.

"All of 'em. Then they won at the tables, had too much to drink to celebrate, and had their keys confiscated by security while the casino staff arranged for their transportation back home. Their cars were retained in a leased lot for thirty days, and then transported to the DMV impound."

"Well, this is tremendous progress," Jacob sat up straight. "So tracking down the involved parties should be easy at this point."

"Well, there's the snag," she replied. "The casino holds contracts with three different transportation companies, but all three deny having driven the victims home on the nights in question."

"What about the staff? One of them must know who picked up these individuals. Unless they're blind or stupid."

She sighed a frustrated sigh. "Remember what I said a few weeks back about the mayor outsourcing the police to provide security for the Marx? Well, turns out that it was members of our own force who escorted our victims from the casino floor to their transportation."

"And they don't know one transportation outfit from another," I mumbled.

"Exactly. And they're all rookies looking for some extra income. And if that isn't enough, from the footage we've reviewed so far, it looks like each time this happened a different officer was on duty."

"You've interviewed them, I hope?" Jacob asked.

"Of course. But they're clueless – no real idea of how security is supposed to work over there. They weren't even able to ID the driver who picked up the victims; they said he was dressed in a dark coat, wore sunglasses, and had a low-brimmed hat."

"And that didn't make them suspicious?"

She snickered. "You'd be surprised how many people in this city match that description." She shrugged. "If it wasn't so gruesome, I'd admire the precision of it all."

"What do you mean?" I asked.

"Think about it. All the elements are there for an untraceable bout of murders. Victims too drunk to know what's going on or defend themselves. A casino that's more interested in outsourcing security than providing it themselves. Different recruits working the floor each night, none with adequate security training. An anonymous driver. And someone who knows all of this and is able to target a victim and coordinate a pickup on just the right night to ensure that the officer on duty hasn't dealt with the driver yet."

Jacob leaned back, thinking it all over. "Sounds like an inside job to me."

Annie nodded reluctantly. "I hate to admit it, but I agree. Things are about to get dirty downtown."

"Well, there is one upside," I spoke up, all eyes immediately upon me. "Since you've got this much figured out, if it *is* an inside job, then the murderer likely won't strike again. And if it isn't, he will and you'll be able to catch him in the act."

Jacob smiled. "Good point."

But Annie was unimpressed with my remarkable observation. "If it's an inside job, I have to be careful."

"What do you mean?" I asked.

"More than one detective has been killed while investigating the crimes of his fellow officers."

That hit me hard. I knew Annie's job was dangerous, and I knew full well that at times her life would be in danger, but I'd always thought of the force as a close-knit group who looked out for each other.

She coughed, patting her chest. "What's taking Larry so long?"

As if on cue, our waiter returned, glass in hand. "I'm sorry about that," he said. "There was a bit of a mix-up in the kitchen."

"It's water, Larry," Annie answered him, annoyed. "It's not difficult."

"Again, I'm sorry," he replied, and vanished once more without another word.

"What's with him?" I asked. "Normally, he's *much* more entertaining. Tonight he seems bothered."

"Whatever," Annie mumbled, reaching into her purse and removing a straw, its top already unwrapped. She held it upright in front of her, tapping it against the table, apparently lost in thought.

"You brought your own straw?" I asked, amused.

"I chipped a tooth," she answered. "I can't drink anything without one until I get it fixed. Where's Freddie tonight?" she changed the subject.

As expected, all eyes turned toward me. But I had come prepared, just in case; no need to guess like I had last time. Freddie wouldn't be showing up this week. I had called him a few days prior to ask.

"He said he couldn't make it," I answered. Although now that I thought about it, I couldn't remember *why* he wouldn't be along. Maybe she wouldn't ask.

"Why not?"

Of course.

I had to come up with something.

Nothing.

But that never stopped me from opening my mouth before.

"He's at a dancing lesson."

Silence.

"You have no idea," Annie finally countered.

"None at all," I admitted.

So at least that was out in the open. Nothing more to do than pick up what remained of my pride and move along.

"What you were saying, Annie," Jacob spoke up again, his forehead lined with concern, "about being careful. Do you think you're in danger?"

She hesitated, then glanced around the dining room. It was still fairly empty, but there were two or three tables occupied besides our own, and a couple of booths. "I don't know," she answered, her voice subdued. "It's probably just paranoia, but I get the feeling that someone is following me."

"Someone?"

"I can't explain it," she went on. "Cars in the rearview, people who look just a little too familiar catching my eye wherever I go."

"Anyone you recognize?" I asked.

She shook her head. "I can't quite put my finger on it. But the whole thing's unnerving."

"Well, paranoia or not, you'd better be careful," Jacob continued. "We've got more than enough brothers in this clan to keep things going if one of us gets knocked off, but we only have one sister."

If the comment was meant to amuse her, she didn't show it. "The worst part is, I don't know who I can trust."

"You can trust us," I offered.

"Of course I can. You're family. But what about everyone else? The killer could be anyone, anywhere. He could be someone each of us sees every single week. He could be right here, right now."

"Right here?" Jacob asked, doubtfully, examining the bottom of his empty cup.

"In this restaurant, I mean."

"If he has bad taste in food, maybe," I answered. "Or the desire to choke on a hairball."

"Why would he be here?" Jacob asked, returning his vacant prize to its proper place.

"Well, why not? Plenty of people come and go in here and we don't know any of them. If someone wanted to keep an eye on me, they'd have an easy enough time blending in."

Jacob shrugged. "Okay, I think that now it's the paranoia talking."

But that didn't deter her. "It could be the manager. The head chef. It could even be *that* guy," she said, nodding in the direction of a nearby booth.

We all turned and looked, but the object of her statement was an older gentleman, eyes weak and hands shaky, barely able to navigate his soup spoon from bowl to mouth without losing half of its contents all over the table. We turned back to our sister to see her smiling slyly, stirring her water glass unconsciously with her straw as she tried not to giggle.

"You can't be serious," Jacob answered her.

"Well, not *him*," she answered. "But anyone."

She lifted her glass, touched the straw to her lips, then made a face, putting the glass down hard once more. "Ugh!"

"What is it?" I asked.

"This water. It's awful."

"Maybe it's your tooth."

"That's stupid."

"Let me taste it," Jacob said, reaching for the glass, but she pulled it away, alarm on her face.

"What?" he asked.

For a moment she seemed at a loss for words, but quickly replied "I don't need your backwash contaminating this any further. Besides," she added, "Larry's our waiter. If anyone should taste it, it should be him."

"Larry!" I yelled out in no direction in particular, and as expected, in an instant his massive girth was leaning precariously overhead, the closest I'd seen him all night, his hands clasped together in true serving form.

"Yes, may I help you?" he asked.

I nodded in the direction of the offending beverage. "Annie seems to think you've contaminated the drinking water."

His face registered sympathetic shock as he shifted his gaze to our sister. "I'm sorry if there's a problem. Would you like another?"

"Yes, I would," she answered, removing her straw and offering up the glass. "But first, I want you to taste this one."

"Excuse me?"

She eyed him a moment. "I would like you to taste the water you brought me. It's disgusting."

He studied her, caught off guard by the unusual request. But apparently the consequence of introducing a bad taste into his mouth was preferable to the negative impact any disagreement on his part would have on the tip, and so, after a few seconds of working out the bottom line, he lifted the glass, examined it closely, and took a small sip.

We watched him with interest, unsure how he would react, and for a moment it seemed a quizzical gaze was all he would give us in reply. But then a look of shock burst upon his face, and his hands rushed to his throat as the glass fell to the floor, shattering as it struck.

We all sat there, frozen in stunned surprise, unable to react. And as we watched, Larry coughed, his eyes wide with alarm. He lost his balance, struck one hand upon the table's edge to right himself, the loud jolt sending beverages spilling onto their sides and silverware jumping into the air, and breaking us from our stunned state. We jumped back, knocking over our chairs in the process.

Larry looked up, his eyes meeting my own, fear in their centers. He opened his mouth, tried to speak, but whatever he said came out as little more than a gurgle, and then he went suddenly limp, his face and chest crashing down upon the table with his full weight, snapping the support and sending all manner of food and dishes flying as he collapsed to the floor between us.

Someone screamed.

Annie dropped to the floor, cradling Larry's head in her hands, her anger now replaced with distress. "Larry!" she cried. "Larry, look at me!"

Jacob looked around for his phone, grabbed it up from the floor, started to dial, then cursed, hurling it to his feet where it splintered to pieces. He spun around, facing the patrons on all sides, and shouted "Someone call an ambulance!" Then to me, "So you tested 911, did you?"

The paramedics showed up just in time. His pulse was already faint when they arrived, and another few minutes and they said his heart would have stopped completely. They couldn't tell us what happened – only after they got him to the hospital would anyone know for sure. But even as they carted him away in the back of the ambulance, the three of us standing in the wash of the flashing lights, we knew the truth.

Larry had been poisoned.

And as bad as that was, that wasn't the worst of it. Because as far as we knew, Larry wasn't the intended target.

Annie was.

# Chapter Six

## May 20th

I knew something was different the moment I stepped into Barlowe's for the evening, although it took me until my arrival at our usual table to realize what it was. The dining room, normally boasting as many empty seats as it did full, was tonight filled to capacity.

"What's going on?" I asked as I sat down.

"I don't know," Jacob answered, irritation in his voice. "But they've been here since I showed up, and as far as I can tell, not a single one has left yet."

"The regulars will be upset," I said, referring to the usual patrons.

"The regulars are already upset," referring to himself.

I looked around. The clientele was varied to say the least. Almost too much so, if such a thing is possible, for it was as if the whole summit were contrived ahead of time and marched through the front doors in a show of diversity.

I had an awful thought.

"They're not activists, are they?"

Jacob shrugged. "If they aren't, they will be by the end of the night. Indigestion can only strike so many people at once before they start picketing."

I snickered. "The chef must be having a nervous breakdown."

"The chef isn't in. None of the usual kitchen staff are. They've been out all week, ever since the incident with Larry."

"Speaking of whom," I looked around, hoping to catch a glance of our usual server, "I wonder how he's doing."

Jacob frowned. "I'm more worried about Annie. Everything she was saying last Thursday, and then the attempt on her life, and after that, Larry. She's been through a lot this week."

"At least she didn't end up in the hospital."

"Yes, there is that." Jacob fumbled with his cup, tapping his fingers on the rim absent-mindedly. "Let me ask you something," he leaned in close. "Last week. Any of that seem...unusual...to you?"

My mouth must have dropped at the question. "You mean, other than Annie's drink being poisoned and Larry taking a nap on the table? No, nothing at all."

"But that's just it. Something isn't adding up, and I can't quite place it." He resumed his tapping, then took a sip. "There's more to this. I'm certain of it."

"Suit yourself," I replied. "I've got better things to worry about tonight."

"Such as?"

"Such as what I should wear next week when my act opens downtown."

"Your act?" For once, Jacob seemed genuinely surprised. "Someone finally picked it up?"

"That's right," I nodded, unable to hold back a smile. "Turns out I've been going about the business of being hilarious all wrong. Instead of building my routine on what I thought would make everyone else laugh, I should have stuck to my own brand of humor all along."

Jacob cocked his head. "I wouldn't have thought that."

"Neither did I. But after months of failing to get a bite, I finally sat down and wrote up a routine based on circumstances I've experienced firsthand."

A worried look entered Jacob's eyes. "I'm not sure I like where this is going."

"Well, it's not so much a routine as it is a performance. A short play, actually."

"A play based on what?"

I smiled, knowing he'd hate the answer. "A dysfunctional family of vampire siblings. I thought I'd tell the story through a series of weekly dinners spent together at a local eatery. I've titled it *The Vampire Diners*. Pretty clever, don't you think?"

"I think," Jacob answered, glaring at me, "that *this* dysfunctional family has enough to worry about already. The last thing we need is you exposing our dinner conversations to total strangers for the sake of a few laughs."

"It's not *all* about the laughs." I thought a moment. "There's also the money. You were the one who told me how it's more important than happiness, remember?"

"And the title could use some work."

"What about *The Vampire Patrons?*" a familiar voice caught my attention, and I looked up to see Freddie.

At least, I thought it was Freddie.

For a moment I really wasn't sure, as he was without any and all elements of disguise for the first time in as long as I could remember.

In other words, he looked normal.

And that *wasn't* normal.

"Freddie?" I greeted him cautiously.

"Jeans and a polo, that's a good look for you," Jacob commented approvingly. "Though I can't say I like the hair."

Truth be told, neither did I. Either Freddie disagreed, or he was intent on not wasting the rest of the gel he'd purchased for his last dinner out, though in my opinion the glitter and makeup had been far less disturbing.

He grinned as he sat down, his uncommonly ordinary appearance putting me on edge, and I posed the question: "What happened?"

"Glad you asked," he replied, swinging himself around sideways in his chair, letting his legs dangle across one arm while he propped himself up with an elbow on the other. "About a week ago I was down at the blood bank, picking up my monthly prescription. As always, I was in character: I had the hair, the makeup, the lame acting, the whole bit. But then something happened. Standing in line with everyone else, I was suddenly struck by how completely out of place I really felt. I mean, there I was, surrounded by vampires, and yet looking and acting like none of them. And do you know why? Because even vampires don't act like vampires – we act like everyone else! That's when it hit me: vampires today are *nothing* like what Hollywood envisioned years ago. We never were, really, but it's only grown more true with time. And I realized just how tired I was of it all: the endless rules, the absurd costumes, the ridiculous behavior. It's degrading."

I stared back at him.

Jacob, too, seemed at a loss, though he eventually gathered his thoughts and cleared his throat. "Um, Freddie, I think you've had a breakthrough."

Freddie only shrugged. "I don't know. Maybe. But I won't be heading down to the costume shop anytime soon." He thought a moment. "Do you realize how much money I'll save? I'm gonna need a new hobby."

That, I had to jump on. "Have you thought about going into acting? You've definitely got the chops for it."

He rolled his eyes. "I'm not going on stage for you."

"Well, I had to ask."

"Where's Annie?" Jacob glanced at his watch. "She's late."

"Not the first time," I replied.

"You wouldn't know. Anyway, she called me a few minutes before you arrived. Said she was on her way. I wonder what's taking her so long."

"Oh, just drink your coffee already. You know, we never order until at least three of us are here anyway, and I'm starved. C'mon – it'll be a novel experience for Freddie."

"You know, it's not like I've never ordered a meal for myself," Freddie spoke up.

"No, but you've never had the pleasure of having Larry tell you what you want, either."

"One problem," Jacob interrupted. "Larry's not here. Do you listen to *anything* I tell you?"

I shrugged. "I drift in and out."

Jacob shook his head, but then his eyes widened. "Of course, I could be wrong."

I turned around to see what had caught his attention, and there I saw Larry himself, striding purposefully into our section with heavy footsteps. He was dressed in his usual serving garb, but the look on his face was one of serious anticipation.

I swallowed hard.

But as he neared us, his eyes grew pleasant and he smiled warmly. "Good evening. I apologize for my tardiness. I trust your service so far this evening has exceeded your expectations?"

Jacob smiled. "Actually, it's merely met them. But now that you're here, I expect that to change."

Larry smiled, showing off his white teeth. "Of course." He glanced around the table, noticing for the first time that Annie was not present. He let out his breath in a sudden burst of air, as if he'd been holding it in until just then.

"You okay?" I asked.

"Hmm? Yes, I'm feeling much better now, thank you."

I squinted up at him, then sent a sideways glance to Jacob, and in an instant I knew he felt it, too. Something wasn't right. True, Larry was nothing if not his usual professional self, his attire to his etiquette spot on, but we'd been served by him for long enough to pick out much more than the superficial pleasantries.

"Larry," Jacob spoke up. "I'm running a little dry here. Would you mind getting me a refill?"

Larry raised his eyebrows inquisitively.

"And a cola for me," I added. "Hold the ice." Sure, as if *that* would prevent last week from repeating itself.

"A coffee and a cola," Larry nodded, then turned to Freddie. "What about you?"

As was quickly becoming his habit, Freddie just shrugged. "Dunno. Bring me whatever you think I want."

Again Larry nodded, then turned and strode briskly out of the dining room.

I looked at Jacob, finding him already looking at me. "What's going on?" I asked.

"I'm not sure," he answered. "Larry's not acting like himself, though."

Silently I agreed, but I was unsure of what to make of it, and before I knew it, our waiter had returned. My cola arrived before me looking both suspicious and refreshing, Freddie's beverage made its appearance in the form of an exotic drink rimmed with sugar and topped with a paper umbrella, and Larry filled Jacob's cup before us all. When he finished, he reached into his side pocket and withdrew several folded napkins, placing them before Jacob and saying, "I thought you might want these."

Jacob nodded, and once more Larry withdrew.

Freddie, holding his glass aloft as he examined it from every angle, asked, "So what did he write on the napkins?"

"I'm about to find out," Jacob answered.

I looked from one to the other. "Ah, what did I miss?"

But Jacob said nothing, and instead casually turned up the corner of the first napkin, then the one underneath, then the one under that. He paused, squinted, and removed the last from the pile, then crumpled it and tossed it aside. Without a word he retrieved his cell, a replacement for his shattered phone of the week before, punched a few buttons, and held it to his ear.

"Jacob," I pressed, but his scowl shushed me as he drummed his fingers anxiously across the table. A moment later and he slapped it shut again, pocketing it once more.

"What is it?" I asked.

"It's Annie," he answered gravely. "And it's too late."

I was about to ask him what was too late when the sound of high-heels caught my attention. Annie had arrived, but she had no more than sat down before Larry was at her side, his hand upon her shoulder. "You have to leave now," he instructed her, insistence in his voice.

"What?" she asked, surprised. "What are you talking about? Please take your hand off me."

"*Now*," he repeated. "You're in danger."

"Larry," I began, "what's all this about?"

He turned his head sharply to me. "That's for your sister to explain. As for me, despite all that's happened, I'm trying to help her." He turned back to Annie, looked her in the eye. "You have to trust me."

But she only shook her head. "I know what you were about to do."

"No, you don't," he replied. "You only thought you did. I wanted to protect you."

"Protect me? From whom?"

He only stared back at her, but Jacob's mind had shifted into overdrive. He'd caught the scent of deception, and when he started to work something out, he rarely failed, though it may take him one or two attempts to iron out all the details. He spoke up suddenly. "Larry cracked the case after all, didn't he, Annie? He figured it out."

Her gaze shifted to him, but she didn't answer.

Jacob continued. "He solved it, but you couldn't stand that. No. Wait. No, it wasn't that. It *scared* you." He grew thoughtful. "Why did it scare you?"

"I don't know what you're talking about," she replied indignantly, shifting in her seat as if attempting to rise, but Larry's hand was still on her shoulder, holding her in place. "You won't even make it out the front door," he whispered harshly. "There are undercovers all over the restaurant. We need to figure this out right here, right now."

"I don't know what you mean!" she insisted.

"Annie," Jacob interrupted, his voice soft yet firm. "There's a time to play dumb. It's called a cross-examination. This is *not* that time. You said you could trust us, that we're family. Now, do you want our help or not?"

She looked from one of us to the next, worry and fear both heavy on her face. "Alright," she said at last. "What do you want?"

"The truth, for starters," Freddie answered, still lounging sideways, hands now folded on his lap. In contrast to the rest of us, he seemed oddly at ease. Maybe it was his new persona. Or any lack of one thereof. I really couldn't be sure, not having seen him as himself in ages.

"Let me tell you what *I* think happened," Jacob continued. "And you can go ahead and play devil's advocate all you want. That way, you're not admitting to anything, and if anyone overhears us, I'm just thinking out loud."

Annie held him in a long stare, then bit her lip and gave a quick nod.

"Very well," Jacob relaxed, sipping and leaning in close. I found myself doing the same. "I must admit I don't know exactly when or how all this started, so I will begin with some speculation."

I noticed immediately his voice had changed. That is, it was serious, but he was keeping his volume unusually tempered, a detail made all the more strange given the bustle of the other patrons on all sides. I nearly asked him to speak up, but then thought the better of it.

"The police investigation into these murders has been one blunder after another, so much so that it defies reason. Even in an incompetent system there are bound to be successes sooner or later, but not here. Instead, it seems that something has hindered the investigation from the very start. Given the broad reach which this influence must require in order to convolute the case at every turn, I must assume that it is the work of an insider. Specifically, someone working on the force."

"Yes," I spoke up. "You've said that before. Tell us something we don't know."

"Alright," he took another sip to wet his tongue. "That person is sitting at this table."

"What?!" I nearly shouted. "Who?"

Freddie rolled his eyes so far back I thought he'd fall out of his chair. "You can't really be that dense, can you? There's only one person at this table who works on the force, so there's only one person here who could be the insider."

I looked at Freddie, then over to Annie. "Annie?"

Jacob nodded. "I'm afraid our sister is the Midnight Mauler."

"Midnight Murderer," Freddie corrected him.

"Midnight Murder*ess*," I corrected Freddie.

"Shut up, all of you," Annie hissed, and for a moment I forgot she was the subject of our debate. She glared at Jacob. "You think *I* did this? Fine. Make your case."

"I intend to," he replied, and I could not help but notice a certain confidence in his words. "Even before Detective Gayton stepped down from the investigation, you had complete access to all evidence, all crime scenes, all personnel. That means you were one of very few individuals able to foil the investigation while also introducing your own clues along the way, the most obvious being the false werewolf fur found at the scene of every crime. Larry's own intuition suggested that it had been planted, and when you had your forensics lab run tests on his control, as he called it, it didn't match with the type of fur found on the victims. Further testing revealed that the bodies were found with traces of wolf fur, not lycan fur. I've seen my share of werewolf murders, and I know your forensics techs would never have made such a gross mistake unless they were intentionally handed falsified evidence or if they were somehow involved in the conspiracy.

"There is also the matter of you being the one person to repeatedly refer to these murders as maulings, and you being the only person to suggest the murderer was a woman. Now, it's true that we all called them maulings when the victims first started making the news, but you should have known better, and your insistence on this key point reinforces your attempts to throw suspicion on the lycans. As to the gender of the person responsible, while you have no doubt attempted to distance yourself from these acts, I believe you have also taken a certain pride in your work as well. Still," he took another sip, "none of this would hold up in court — it is all much too speculative."

Already my own mind was spinning. If this was mere speculation, then surely when he trotted out the hard facts I'd fall out of my chair. I looked around for a soft place to land.

Jacob continued. "Beyond conjecture, I find it troubling that both the victims and the conditions of the murders were so keenly chosen. The victims because they were older, celebrating, and drunk, and were, therefore, both defenseless and unable to take the stand should they somehow survive an attack, having no real idea what happened, and the conditions because on each occasion a different officer was providing security for the casino, and was a rookie besides. This allowed for a pickup by an unmarked car without arising suspicion. The officers wouldn't have known they just delivered the next victim directly into the murderer's hands, and because a different member of the force was on duty each night, they would never have grown suspicious of the same car and driver making the rounds. I imagine few department members have access to this sort of scheduling information, but weeks ago you seemed to know more than enough. With a little care, you could have selected your times and victims perfectly.

"And while we're on the topic, let's talk about your car. It's an unmarked department vehicle, perfect for anonymous pickups and blending into traffic, especially at night. It also has a leather interior, one with a smell you claim you can't stand, and so you keep plastic over the backseat, hang more than a few air fresheners up front, and keep the windows rolled down even when it's freezing out. More likely you're trying to keep blood off the upholstery and airing out the car during the day to rid it of the smell of dead bodies. I wonder what your forensics team would find if they performed a sweep of the interior. One or two bits of damning evidence, I'm sure."

He paused, taking another drink and eyeing her closely. "Then there's the poisoning incident just last week. I'd guess you wanted it to look like someone was trying to poison *you*, most likely to further the illusion that you were getting close to cracking the case yourself, but in reality you were trying to silence Larry here, who had figured it all out and even had the decency to tell you. But you didn't trust him. You thought he was going to turn you in, and so you chose to kill him instead."

"Wait," I interrupted. "Larry brought the water out to Annie. She was the one who complained about the taste and gave it back to him."

"Yes, she did," Jacob replied. "But she also insisted that he taste it for himself. Now think back – what did Annie do just before she took a drink?"

I thought back. Not surprisingly, nothing was waiting for me when I got there.

"She retrieved a straw from her purse," Jacob continued, "a straw already unwrapped at one end, its *top* end. Why? Because there was something inside of it. Then she tapped it on the table, solidifying its contents. While doing that she made a comment about a gentleman at a nearby booth, something which drew our attention away from her, and the next thing you know she's stirring her water glass with the very same straw. This begs the question: What was in it?"

"I can answer that," Larry chimed in. "The doctors at the hospital told me I had been poisoned with silver nitrate."

"Silver nitrate," Jacob smiled. "After Larry emailed you to tell you he'd figured out what you were doing, you began sending yourself lab data, mainly information on chemicals used in forensic examinations.

Among those was silver nitrate, commonly used to reveal latent fingerprints in crime scenes. It was a good choice, as it dissolves in water and poses little risk to humans and vampires in small doses, but is lethal to werewolves even in miniscule amounts. It was also something to which you would have had easy access. And with your straw, you both had a simple way of delivering the poison without suspicion into your own glass, as well as simulating the consumption of the water yourself. There was only a single obvious error in your ruse: Why would anyone try to poison a vampire using silver nitrate in the first place? It doesn't make any sense. Even if you *had* taken a full drink from the glass, you would have ended up with a minor case of indigestion at most. Any gumshoe worth his salt could have deduced the poison wasn't meant for you. And I wonder: If we took a look in your mouth, would we find the chipped tooth that supposedly warranted the straw in the first place?"

Again he fell silent. I was doing what I could to keep up, but it seemed he was rattling off more of a web of facts and speculation than a simple, clean-cut case. I looked over at Freddie, who was nodding and watching the whole thing with interest and relaxed as ever, and then back to Annie, her face less shocked now than it was defeated, with tears welling in the corners of her eyes, and Larry standing ever above, his hand still upon her shoulder, though now more of a comfort than a restraint.

"Of course, the biggest question," Jacob finally broke the silence, "is why?"

At that Annie looked slowly around the table, her gaze crossing each of us, even Larry, until it finally came to rest upon our oldest brother. "Because I'm a second-class citizen," she answered. "We're *all* second-class citizens, and no matter what we do or how good we do it, we'll never get ahead in the world like the humans do. This was my only chance to move ahead in the department, to move ahead at all, not by locking up thieves and rapists and murderers, but by solving the single greatest mass murdering case in the history of this city. If I solved *this* crime, then for once in my life maybe it wouldn't matter that I was a vampire. Maybe I'd finally get the respect that any human doing my job would have gotten a long time ago."

Jacob nodded thoughtfully. He almost looked sympathetic. "You know," he said, "Larry tried to keep you from showing up here tonight. He slipped me a note before you arrived, telling me to keep you away. He knew what you were walking into."

She looked back up at Larry, already looking down at her, a sad giant of a man. "I know you were scared," he said softly. "I know why you did what you did, to the others and to me. It changes nothing." Slowly he stooped down, kneeling beside her, though his massive build afforded him no trouble to look deep into her eyes. "I love you, Annie. I've always loved you. And I will no matter what happens next."

At that, our sister let fall a single tear silently to the floor, and she placed her palm against his cheek. "Larry..." she whispered.

"But you must know," he continued solemnly, "that I wasn't working alone."

That killed the moment right then and there, and she withdrew, shrinking away. "What do you mean?"

"I'll tell you what he means," an unfamiliar voice rose above the clamor, and I turned to see a tall man in a black suit standing not ten feet from us and watching us keenly. He was flanked by two officers, and a gold badge shone from his belt. Annie's eyes darkened when she saw him. "Gayton," she hissed.

"I'm afraid so," he announced, swaggering proudly forward as he looked us over, chuckling. "And you thought I was off the case. If only you knew how close we were watching you all along."

Annie jumped out of her chair, her sudden jolt catching Larry off guard as she broke free. She stood on one side of our table, Gayton and his boys on the other, the rest of us caught between. Annie glared at the newcomer. "Gayton, I'll —"

"You'll what?" he sneered. "Kill me too? I don't think so."

She made a sudden grab for something under her arm, but the detective was faster, and before she could draw her gun, he already had his aimed at her chest. "Don't," he said sternly.

She withdrew her hand gradually, then raised both as she took a single step back.

"*Don't*," Gayton repeated, and she froze in place.

Slowly Larry rose from his seat, gaining his full height beside the table, standing his ground between our sister and the law. "Annie."

"What?!" she demanded, angry and desperate. "You were working with them this whole time? Against me?"

His face fell. "Like you said, we're *all* second-class citizens."

"Larry here has been invaluable to us," Gayton remarked, gesturing fondly to our waiter. "We approached him several months ago, when we were first starting to suspect your loyalties. We made him an offer of full citizenship if he came through for us." The detective sent an admiring gaze in Larry's direction. "And he has."

"Annie," Larry tried again, "I tried to warn you. I didn't want this to happen."

"Didn't you? You tell me you love me, and then you turn around and do *this*?"

He smiled a sad smile and shook his head. "No. I told you I loved you. And to prove it, I'm doing *this*."

And without any warning he spun suddenly about and let loose a horrific scream, a guttural blast both growl and shout, and as the whole of the dining room fell into sudden silence, he lunged.

Gayton and his sidekicks went down hard, but the fight was only beginning, and as the detective employed his weapon, Larry was barely able to knock it from its mark before a shot rang out, striking the ceiling above with a crack.

The werewolf looked over his shoulder, his face a twisted combination of animal and man, his eyes alive with primal rage. "Go!" he shouted, but Annie remained fixed, both shock and awe planting her feet where she stood.

Another shot, and again Larry shouted. "Get her out of here!"

Jacob stood, reached out to her, and grasped her shoulder. Their eyes met for an instant, and then she turned and ran for the kitchen, as well as the back door.

Larry and the boys were still wrestling on the floor, and seeing their guns knocked out of reach, I suddenly found the whole scuffle rather comical. Larry would go down, but then he was back up again and walloping back two of his assailants in the process, then the third would jump on him from behind and he'd spin around, tossing the attacker into a nearby booth. Then the other two would rush and he'd go down again, only to come up a moment later holding one over his head while he punted the other away like a football.

By now I was on my feet as well, my own adrenaline urging me to join in while every sane part advised against it. Left and right the undercover officers were jumping up from their dinners to defend their commanding officer, but just as quickly they found themselves greeted by the fists and boots of the remaining patrons, now springing from their own meals to intervene. In under a minute, the restaurant had turned into an all-out brawl.

Freddie appeared at my side. Against all odds of getting a straight reply, I offered up the one question on my mind. "What *exactly* is going on here?"

"You mean the scrappers? They're friends of mine. Activists."

I looked at him, more than a little amused. "You're kidding!"

"Every one of them, I swear."

I took another look around the dining room. "So what are they activist'ing against, exactly?"

"At the moment? Detective Gayton and his merry men," Jacob answered, appearing on my other hand, cup still in hand. He gave us a sideways glance. "I'm generally not a fan of protesters, but I have to give them credit: they've got moxie. Might even be affiliated with PETA."

"I don't know," I replied as I took in the throng of black eyes and flying teeth. "They've got an awful lot of clothes on."

"They're *political* activists," Freddie corrected.

Jacob nodded, sipping his coffee. "That's probably better for Larry anyway, assuming he makes it out of this. I doubt very much his dignity could take the thought of animal activists saving his hide."

"So what're they doing *here*?" I asked.

"I invited them," Freddie replied. "I heard they'd be in town this week for some rallies downtown – I'm friends with a few and they needed a place to stay – so I arranged for a few dozen to show up for dinner tonight in case things got ugly."

Jacob coughed, spraying coffee out his mouth and onto the floor. "You knew this was going to happen?"

Freddie laughed. "Jacob, I had this case cracked wide open weeks ago. I was just waiting to see if the rest of you would get wise before I spilled the beans. Tonight was going to be the night. Mind you," he added, "I had no idea Gayton would be making an appearance."

"Wait," I interrupted. "If you didn't know Gayton was coming, then why the cavalry in the first place?"

"Because I had no idea how Annie would react. I already knew she was willing to poison someone to avoid getting caught; who knows what she'd have done to keep *me* quiet. And there's Larry; we've all seen the way he looks at her. He'd do anything for that girl. I imagined myself running for the parking lot with an armed cop and a lovestruck waiter on my tail. I needed a way to even the odds."

"So these friends of yours," I gestured in the general direction of the chaos. "They do realize you're in no danger and they'll be spending the night in jail?"

He grinned again. "Oh, I doubt they really showed up to protect me; they love this sort of thing. They don't mind getting their hands dirty if it means making the front page."

"Political activists, you said," Jacob spoke up. "What are they in town to rally against?"

"Primarily the mayor's awarding of city contracts to friends and political allies."

"Really?" My brother's eyes sparkled. "Maybe they're not so bad after all."

"And his ties to several crime bosses in the area."

"They can share my restaurant anytime."

"And our corrupt judicial system."

"A bunch of worthless bums, all of them."

The commotion went on for several minutes more, but as quickly as it started, the fray died, and the restaurant was returned to its normal atmosphere, albeit one with the added chaos of broken tables and chairs, smashed windows, and a few dozen beat-up activists and police lying in all directions across the dining room floor.

As for Larry, he was nowhere to be found, and Annie was by now long gone. I smiled a little. In spite of the evening's awful revelations, the two had made it out.

But we weren't off the hook yet.

Detective Gayton rose to his feet from out of the bruised rabble, suit torn and stained with food and drinks. And as an added insult, what had earlier passed for his hair was now revealed to be a disheveled toupee. It would never be the same.

He crossed the floor in our direction, stumbled over one of his lackeys and lost his balance, but managed to maintain his footing and continued to approach.

"You fool!" he shrieked at Jacob. "You let her get away! I could have you arrested for this!"

"You could," Jacob replied coolly. "And I could sue you for wrongful prosecution with a side of harassment."

Gayton's face turned red, and his voice rose higher still. "You're a lawyer, for cryin' out loud! I don't care if she's your sister or not! You're supposed to uphold the law! *Do your job!*"

"My dear Detective, I am quite aware of my profession, as perhaps you should be more aware of yours." He took a long sip from his cup, then met Gayton's eyes in a dark stare. "I *will* do my job. But first, you have to bring her to court."

The two locked eyes for a moment, and then the detective stormed off toward the front door, cursing under his breath as he went. "And, Detective," Jacob called out after him, to which he stopped in midstep and spun about to face us one last time, "I wouldn't go walking down any dark alleys anytime soon if I were you."

# ⁐ EPILOGUE ⁐

I began tonight's narrative by stating an obvious but often-overlooked truth: that, of course, being that the single greatest misconception held by the general public concerning vampires is that we can't appreciate a good joke. I hope that I have now, in some small way, managed to discredit this notion in the minds of all present. But even if in this single undertaking I have failed, rest assured that your applause and the price you paid for admission this evening are consolation enough for me.

As for the subjects of the tale, I confess I have taken some liberties, bending the facts and muddying the depictions of our evenings together. In an ideal world they would thank me for reducing their individual quirks to near-normal levels, proof for the optimists among you that our world is far from ideal.

That observation aside, I believe that now is the point at which I'm supposed to give an accounting of the individuals on whom the characters of this satire were based. I do this not for their own benefit, but rather to grant to this most discerning and sophisticated audience of theatergoers a glimpse into their lives without the bias of the tale itself.

Larry is still waiting tables at Barlowe's, having never dreamt of doing anything as reckless as tackling an armed detective and two law officers and instigating a restaurant-wide brawl to give a mass murderess the opportunity to escape justice. As for his romantic interests, I can't say much – the only intimacy I've ever known a vampire and werewolf to share is that of tooth and claw, and such relationships tend to fail the moment one gains the upper hand over the other. On a final note, I should point out that Larry *is* every bit as quick-witted as I suggested, a quality that finds him often looking down the business end of a dead-end case that has my sister stumped.

Speaking of Annie, I would be remiss if I failed to mention that she didn't *really* commit all those murders, having suffered her whole life with chronic niceness, and Jacob didn't single-handedly make sense of five weeks' worth of clues in under five minutes, having suffered most of his life with deductive incompetence. And while Freddie did briefly break from his obsession with Hollywood vampires, in no time at all he was back at it, making scenes over dinner and entertaining the rest of us in the process.

As for me, it goes without saying I broke into comedy after all, though not quite in the way I intended. Truth be told, I'd always imagined myself telling stand-up in clubs packed wall-to-wall with adoring fans, not giving live epilogues to audiences of stunned theatergoers – your vacant stares are understandable, by the way, and a completely normal reaction to such symphonic blending of literary culture and comedic satire – but it turns out writing plays is much less bothersome than conjuring up stand-up routines, especially when one considers the endless source of material in whose company I have the unfortunate obligation to dine every Thursday night.

They say the secret of a good comedy is telling the truth. I must agree, though it probably doesn't hurt to toss in a werewolf and a few vampires for good measure.

Probably.

www.ingramcontent.com/pod-product-compliance
Lightning Source LLC
Chambersburg PA
CBHW020629130626
46552CB00003B/1146